CITRINE

A Grandmother's Rings Romance

Other Books in *A Grandmother's
Rings Romance* Series:

Sapphire
Amethyst

Other Available Books by Kathryn Quick:

'Tis the Season
Falling for You
Stealing April's Heart
Jessie's Wedding
Blue Diamond

CITRINE

•

Kathryn Quick

AVALON BOOKS
NEW YORK

Published by Thomas Bouregy & Co., Inc.
160 Madison Avenue, New York, NY 10016

Library of Congress Cataloging-in-Publication Data

Quick, Kathryn.
    Citrine / Kathryn Quick.
        p. cm. — (A grandmother's rings romance)
    ISBN 978-0-8034-7772-8 (acid-free paper)
    I. Title.

PS3567.U2935C58 2010
813'.54—dc22
                                            2010006514

PRINTED IN THE UNITED STATES OF AMERICA
ON ACID-FREE PAPER
BY HADDON CRAFTSMEN, BLOOMSBURG, PENNSYLVANIA

For Mom

Special thanks to Caridad Pineiro Scordato, Gail Free-man, Rayna Vause, Melinda Leigh, Anne Walradt and Lois Winston, the founding members of LSFW, and the reason I still write. It's been the best journey ever!

Chapter One

You can't pick your relatives.

Ali Archer's blue-eyed gaze zeroed in on her brother, Trent, among all the guests milling about in the backyard of her sister's house in Westfield, New Jersey.

"Traitor!" she called out as soon as they made eye contact. "Don't even pretend you don't hear me." She put him in her sights and strode straight to him, like a laser beam focused on a mark. Her hands rested on her hips, in case there were still any question of just how determined she was.

Trent Archer nodded in benign recognition and calmly continued to flip the burgers on the built-in barbeque. He waited until she was right next to him before he slid the stainless steel spatula under one of the burgers and raised it to eye level. "Rare or well?" he asked.

A slow grin spread across Ali's lips. When it reached full smirk, she reached out with her forefinger and flicked the edge of the spatula just enough to send the burger flying onto the apron Trent was wearing.

"Just how I like it," she said as she watched it slide down the front of the white cotton fabric and land on Trent's tennis shoes. "Red and juicy."

"Ma!" Trent shouted over his shoulder. "Mooch is here!"

Tess Archer came out the French doors leading to the patio from the family room of her married daughter's house. "Ali, you're late." She watched Trent stab at the fallen burger with a long-handled fork. "What happened?"

"Tragic cooking accident," Ali volunteered. "Where are Somer, Nick, and my nephew?" she asked her mom.

"Inside. Michael woke up from his nap a few minutes ago."

"Great. Lead the way," Ali told her mom. When Tess stepped back inside the house, Ali turned her head to her brother. She shot him an exaggerated smile and said, "Beef-brown is definitely your color."

Trent responded by whispering, "Payback will be coming."

The guests near the grill had witnessed the exchange. They stood, empty plates in hand, with confusion on their faces. Trent waved off their bewilderment. "My sister," he explained as he scooped a well-done burger onto the nearest plate. "She's a little upset with me right now, but she'll be fine." Then he looked around the yard, intent on locating his fiancée. "Linda," he called out when he saw her, "stay close. Mooch is here and she's really mad."

"What was that all about, dear?" Tess asked Ali as they walked through the family room.

Ali's exasperated sigh underscored her frustration. "You know very well what that was all about, Mom."

Tess stopped and turned toward her daughter. "Are you still upset that Trent and Linda got engaged?"

"Of course I'm not upset. I was never upset about Trent's engagement. I love my brother. I want him to be happy. Linda is perfect for him."

Tess brushed Ali's hair from her face just as she did so many times when Ali was a child. "I think so too. Maybe Linda will ask you to be in the wedding party just like Somer did."

Ali waved off her mother's comment. "No." Her tone was emphatic. "I'll have no more of that."

"But Trent met Linda at Somer and Nick's wedding. Maybe you can meet someone. . . ."

"Mother," Ali warned, shaking her head.

"I was just going to say . . ."

"I know what you were going to say," Ali interrupted. "I really just want to see my nephew."

As Ali followed Tess upstairs, her mind filled with conflicting thoughts. It wasn't that she didn't love her sister and brother-in-law. On the contrary, she loved Somer a lot; Nick also. And she was thrilled about her new nephew.

But Trent—she loved him as any sister would love a pain-in-the-neck big brother, but he had broken a solemn sibling pact made to stand strong against a curse put on them by their mother.

Okay, maybe it wasn't a curse in the strictest sense of the word. It was more like a suggestion that they take their grandmother's rings and find their soul mates so Tess could have grandchildren soon.

At first she, Somer, and Trent had taken the rings—an amethyst for Somer, a sapphire for Trent, and a citrine for her—and scoffed at the idea that the rings could make them do anything. But as though under the spell of some type of love voodoo, Ali watched her siblings fall one at a time.

First Somer met Nick Daultry, and before long they were engaged. Then Trent met Linda Wolff at Somer and Trent's wedding, and he fell harder and faster than a cannonball dropped from a bridge.

If all that hadn't been enough pressure for her, now, a little after their second wedding anniversary, Somer and Nick had given Tess her first grandchild, and Trent was engaged to Linda.

Now she was the last one standing.

"I thought I heard a lot of noise," Nick said, coming out of the last room on the right when Tess and Ali got to the top of the stairs. He hugged Ali while Tess went into the nursery ahead of them. "Somer's been waiting for you," he continued.

Ali kissed Nick's cheek. "Now you went and did it. There'll be no stopping Mom now that she's had her first grandchild. She's going to be on me to find a husband like white is on rice."

Nick laughed. "There's always Leonard Wilkenstats."

Ali chuckled. "Naw. He dumped me for a PhD from Princeton. I heard he and Lolly were planning a spring wedding. Good thing I introduced them after Somer's wedding. Humm," she said, tapping her forefinger on her chin. "Do you think I could convince Mom that she made that match?"

Nick shook his head. "I don't think so. But I do think Linda and Trent's wedding will distract her for a little while and buy you some time." A soft baby's cry from inside the room lifted Nick's attention from Ali. "I think my son is calling us," he said, pride clearly in his voice.

Inside the nursery, Tess had just finished changing the baby. She turned when Ali and Nick entered the room and handed Michael to his father. Tucking the infant into the crook of his arm with his hand firmly underneath Michael's little backside, Nick held his son like a piece of spun sugar. Ali could not imagine a more perfect picture.

Nick's free hand caressed his son's cheek when he turned to Ali. "Want to hold him?"

Ali reached out her arms. "Of course I do. You don't think I came all the way to Westfield to see you, do you?" She took Michael from Nick and felt like someone had just handed her an angel.

Somer draped a blue receiving blanket over Ali's right shoulder. "Take this just in case. He just finished his bottle."

Ali smiled at her sister and then turned her attention back to Michael. She inhaled the scent that only comes with babies. Could there be anything that smelled better? At this moment, she couldn't think of one thing.

Michael's blue eyes held hers, and Ali cooed at him until he smiled. "He is so cute." She looked at Nick and Somer. "But I don't understand why you named him Michael."

Somer looked at her son over Ali's shoulder, pride and love shining in her eyes. "We both liked that name."

"But you broke the family tradition of naming the children after the place they were planned, like Mom did—Somerville, Trenton. . . ."

"Don't forget Allamuchy," Nick chimed in.

Tess puckered her lips in lighthearted warning to her son-in-law. "It was the seventies—the days of flower power, peace, and love."

"Yeah, and it was the days of weird names," Ali offered. Michael began to whimper, so she stood and held him against her chest, patting him on his back. "I think a better name would have been something like Garage." She looked at the strange expression on her sister's face and nodded with the satisfaction of getting the exact reaction she wanted. "Yes, little Garage Daultry would have been a perfectly fitting name for this little guy."

Three voices blended at the same time, seemingly in horror. "Garage?"

Michael began to wail. Somer held out her hands. "See, you scared the baby!" Reluctantly, Ali turned Michael over to his mother.

"How on earth did you come up with that one?" Nick asked, watching as his wife rocked Michael in the side-to-side motion mothers seem to do almost on instinct when they have a baby in their arms. He smiled when Michael quieted almost immediately.

"I came up with it because I can count," Ali returned. "And if you calculate backward from Michael's birthday, you get Thanksgiving Day." She walked over to her sister and ran her finger down Michael's cheek before turning back toward Nick. "We had a houseful of company, cousins galore, most of them under the age of ten. After dinner, Mom asked you and Somer to get the pie out of the spare refrigerator—remember?"

Nick began to grin. "Yes, I do."

"You guys came back with the pie, and the conversation over coffee and dessert turned to children"—Ali spun on her heels and pointed to Michael—"and to babies. Nine months later, Michael shows up." She waggled her finger in the air. "And just where was that refrigerator, brother-in-law dear?"

Nick's smile broke wide just before he burst out laughing. "It was in the garage."

Ali threw up her hands. "I rest my case."

"Next corner make a right. The house is five doors down on the left."

Jake Daultry looked out the passenger window of his friend's car and enjoyed the view of the neighborhood. Trees edged a street lined with two-story houses and a couple of kids rode bikes down the sidewalk. He was home.

Well, it wasn't home exactly, but it was the next-best thing: thirty days on leave, with the first stop being at his cousin's house, before another tour of duty in the Middle East. There was no sand, no bullets, and the temperature was under 100. No, it wasn't home, but it was heaven as far as he was concerned.

"Tell me again why you are stopping here before going home?" Tom Davis, the driver of the car and another soldier also on leave, drawled.

Jake took off his aviator sunglasses. The bright September sunlight poured in through the windshield and felt warm on his face—not desert-warm, just warm enough to be pleasant. "Everyone's here," he replied. "My cousin and his wife just had their first, and the family came down for the christening. After a visit, Mom and I will drive home together."

Tom flicked on the blinker and took the car on a lazy turn onto Elm Street. "Aren't you afraid your homecoming is going to upstage the baby?"

Jake shook his head. "That could never happen. Babies are big business in the Daultry family. No one upstages them."

Tom grinned. "Do you mean to tell me that not even a real-life, bona-fide, medal-winning hero could steal a baby's thunder?"

Jake returned the grin and shrugged. "Hey, I was just doing my job."

"Modesty like that might get you a date with the ladies, but it does nothing for me."

"Thanks, but I don't need any help with the ladies," Jake returned confidently.

"Well, I guess you must impress them in your dreams, then, Daultry."

Laughing, Jake angled the rearview mirror so he could see himself in it. "I believe you're jealous, Lieutenant."

"What would I have to be jealous of?" Tom asked, moving the mirror back.

"I'm single, good-looking as heck, and have my pick of all the ladies I want at the O Club."

With a sharp laugh, Tom pulled over to the curb. "Word's out that you don't leave with any of them anyway. I think that maybe you've been stuck in the sand so long you've forgotten what the ladies even want."

With a sharp laugh, Jake dismissed the comment. "And I think you should more worry about what HTs are doing and less about what I do at the O Club."

"I can handle the hard targets just as well as you can. It's the ladies that are in question."

"I do just fine with the opposite sex," Jake returned, "no matter what the chatter might be to the contrary."

"Let's have a challenge then," Tom said, angling his body toward Jake.

Jake leaned back in the seat. "No, let's not have a challenge today. We're not at Delta Base, and it's my first full day back on U.S. soil. All I want to do is enjoy wearing a pair of blue jeans instead of a green flight suit."

Tom nodded. "That's exactly what I had in mind."

Keeping contact with the molded headrest of the rental car, Jake turned his head toward Tom. "What is that sun-baked mind of yours up to?"

Tom uncurled his forefinger from around the steering wheel and pointed. "Now there's a pair of jeans any man could enjoy. Are you game?"

Swiveling his head to follow where Tom gestured, Jake saw what his fellow soldier meant. A few cars down was the cutest pair of jeans he had ever seen. The blue denim curved in and out in all the right places, including a pair of long slender legs. He leaned forward trying to see more, but the rest of the woman seemed to be inside the trunk of a Honda Civic struggling with something she wanted outside awfully bad.

"Think you could sweet talk the owner of those jeans into easing you back into civilian life for a few days?" Tom asked in a playful, suggestive tone, the look in his eyes daring Jack to take him up on the challenge.

The idea was provocative, and Jake mulled it over for a few minutes before answering. "There's no way for you to know if I could. You're not staying."

"We'll be under the honor code," Tom replied without hesitation, "just like in the Academy. You can't lie. You can't cheat." He held out his hand. "What do you say, Captain? Lock and load, and report back in a few days?"

"Or what do I owe you?"

"Or you get me a date with the blond nurse I saw you walk into the O Club the last day you were in the sandbox."

"Which one? There are a lot of blond nurses in Fallujah."

"I want the one I heard invited you to cool your feet in the blow-up pool the nurses have next to their tent."

Jake nodded knowingly and didn't hesitate this time. "Okay, it's a deal." He shook Tom's hand firmly.

"And I'll need a full report on how you sweet-talked her, to prove it," Davis said.

"You'll get a full report, Lieutenant," Jake agreed before getting out of the car and grabbing his green duffel bag out of the back seat. He slammed the back car door and then leaned in the passenger-side window. "I'll even bring you pictures," he said before straightening and patting the hood of the car in a parting gesture.

He watched the car drive away and slung the duffel over his shoulder. Then he spun on his heel, aiming himself at his target. "Eleven months in the sandbox is a long time. I hope I'm not too much out of practice."

Chapter Two

This will work out just fine, Jake said to himself as he approached the car. He watched the woman back out of the trunk and stand, hand on hip, looking at an impossibly huge gift-wrapped box that was apparently stuck inside.

She was slender, but not too thin, judging by the way she filled out the blue jeans. She wore a light pink top that complemented unruly red hair streaked with blond.

He stopped about five feet away from her and set down his duffel bag. He was close enough to see her profile with its finely sculpted nose and flushed cheeks. She turned to look at him, and her large, vivid blue eyes made his heart begin a hard, unrelenting beat.

Suddenly he felt nervous. Imagine that—him, nervous! At age thirty-five, he knew how to get a woman's attention. But he had made this one into a game, something he would normally never think of doing. Why had he let Davis goad him into it?

Because Davis tossed in the Academy honor code,

that's why, Jake answered for himself. Yep, there was nothing more macho than West Pointers on leave trying to outdo each other. For a moment he thought about letting Davis win, but the woman turned fully toward him and crossed her arms over her chest. She pursed her full lips, and his pulse jagged like a bullet ricocheting in a tin can.

"What are you staring at?" she asked. "You never saw someone trying to get something out of a trunk before?"

For a moment, just from looking at the way her hair tumbled around her small shoulders, it seemed as though he'd lost his ability to speak. Silky strands of red and honey blond curved into crescents against her top. The bangs across her smooth forehead emphasized her thickly lashed eyes. *Part girl, part woman,* he thought as he stared at her, wondering which one he was reacting to.

She walked over to him and snapped her fingers in front of his face. "Are you mute or something?"

Jake gave his head a small shake. "No, I can talk."

"But can you carry things?"

"Yeah."

"Then how about making yourself useful and helping me get a box out of my trunk?"

Jake tossed his head. "Sure, I'm always ready to rescue a damsel in distress."

He started to walk to her car when she stopped him with a hand to his chest. "Damsel in distress is a bit extreme, isn't it—I mean, unless you're Dudley Do-Right and I'm tied to a railroad track, that is? Normally I wouldn't need help, but the darn thing got stuck in there somehow."

Jake raised his hands in a don't-shoot pose. "I was only making conversation."

"Less talking and more doing would be better."

By the curve her of mouth and the fire in her eyes, you would have thought that he'd said something horrible to her instead of agreed to help her. His mind whirled with a politically correct response to her gibe. Myth said that red-haired women could turn into screeching harpies when confronted sometimes, but, to him, unpredictability was their allure. They reminded him of the jets he had trained on before becoming a Black Hawk pilot. When he'd flown the F-16 to the edge of the envelope, he'd tested its strengths and weaknesses, but had never really known it until he pushed too far. He sort of felt that way right now.

"Sorry, ma'am," Jake said. "I meant nothing by it."

She dropped her hand and crossed her arms over her chest. "Did I hear you call me 'ma'am'? Just how old do you think I look?"

"Well, let's see now." He stepped back and gave her a lazy once-over intended to make her wonder exactly what he was looking at, but instead he only succeeded in making his own interest in her rise as he took in every attractive line and angle. He could feel a wide grin rise to his face. This red-haired harpy was getting under his skin, and he didn't mind it at all. "I'd say twenty-five," he finally said.

"Twenty-eight," she corrected, "Which makes me way too young to be a ma'am."

"A lady is never too young to be shown respect," Jake replied without an instant of hesitation.

"Call me Ali, then," she said.

"Huh?"

"My name's Ali."

"Well then, Ali, what has you so annoyed today?"

"Who says I'm annoyed?"

"I do, and by the looks of you, so would anyone in a ten-mile radius."

Ali walked back to her car and looked in the side mirror. "What's wrong with the way I look?"

The question made Jake's gaze sweep her form once more. There was absolutely nothing wrong with the way she looked. He would probably remember every vivid detail, but that's not what she wanted to hear right now.

He walked to her as he spoke. "Your cheeks are flushed, your voice is probably an octave too high when you speak, and your body language says I'd better be ready to move back at a moment's notice."

Ali grimaced. "That bad, huh?"

Jake just nodded.

"Okay," Ali said, leaning her backside against the driver's-side door, "I'm probably never going to see you again after today so I'll tell you why I'm annoyed."

"You may see me again sometime," Jake corrected. "People's paths cross all the time."

"I'll chance it," she replied immediately. "Besides, I was rude and you deserve an explanation." She hesitated and shifted her eyes, as she second-guessed whether or not she should continue. "I normally don't give away family secrets to strangers," she explained, "but maybe a neutral perspective might help me get a handle on this thing that's been bugging me for a while."

"Or not, but now I'm intrigued, so I want to know. What is it?"

Ali took a deep breath and then held nothing back. "Fact is, my mother wants me to give her grandchildren."

Jake took a step backward and held up his hands again. "I barely know you."

Ali rolled her eyes. "I don't mean right now, and I don't mean with you. I mean sometime in the future."

"I guess every woman wants that from her children."

"Yes, but my mom is on a mission. My sister and brother have already fallen victims to her curse, and I'm next."

"A curse, you say?" One of Jake's eyebrows rose with the question.

"I know it sounds crazy, but it's true. Mom called a family meeting and gave us these rings, and before you knew it my older sister met this cop and got married, my brother is getting married, and my sister and her husband had a baby. I tell you, Mom unleashed some kind of un-stoppable Cupid-like force when she gave us those rings."

"That's quite a story."

Ali could hear the skepticism in Jake's voice. "It isn't a story," she insisted. "It's a Stephen King novel, and I'm the only person left alive."

"Are your brother and sister happy?"

"Yes, they are."

"Then, what's so bad about it?"

Ali's eyes widened. "Were you not listening?" She pointed to herself with both forefingers, stabbing the air as she spoke. "I . . . am . . . doomed." She began to pace. "I have this strange feeling something's going to happen—like when you're watching a horror film and the heroine is walking up to the spooky, old house. You're screaming to her 'don't go in there,' but she goes in anyway, and wham! The next thing you know the vampire is chewing on her neck."

Jake nearly burst out laughing at the look of terror on her face. "It's daylight. No self-respecting vampire would be up yet."

She dropped her shoulders and sighed. "It was an analogy."

"Don't you want to get married someday?" Jake asked, trying hard not to laugh at her protests.

"Someday—maybe—but not because of some family curse." She saw him cover his mouth to smother a grin. "Never mind. Why did I even tell you anyway?" She swiped at the air with her hand. "You could never understand the power of those rings unless you saw it in action. I swear my grandmother must have been a gypsy." She took two steps away and then came back. "But the fact remains, I have to get the box out of the trunk and into my sister's house. So, Mr. Knight-in-Shinning-Armor, are you still going to help me?"

"The name's Jake," he replied.

Ali nodded. "Okay, Jake then—so how about that box?" she asked, hitching her thumb over her shoulder at the car.

He gave a little bow and smiled. "Your wish is my command—as long as it doesn't mean that we're engaged."

"Oh, you're very funny." Sarcasm laced her voice. "Just help me get it out, and then you're free to go."

Jake walked to the back of the car, thoughts racing through his mind. Should he tell her that they were going to the same party? Naw, he quickly answered himself. It would be much more fun to let this redheaded spitfire find out for herself and see what happened when she did. He just needed to make sure he was out of the line of fire.

He got about a step from the trunk and stopped. "What's in there anyway?"

"It's a gift for my new nephew. He was christened today."

"What is it—a tank?"

"No, it's a drum set."

Jake's eyebrows furrowed. "The little guy can't be more than a few months old." He watched a devious expression race across Ali's face.

"It's payback for my sister starting all this, and I intend to add a piece every year for his birthday until he has a percussion section the size of the Philharmonic's."

"Isn't that a little extreme?"

"No, in my family, it's expected."

"Wow, it must be something at your house on holidays."

"You would not believe me if I told you."

Jake leaned into the trunk. He tugged at the box. It didn't move very much. "You got this in here somehow, so we should be able to get it out," he said, rocking the box back and forth.

Ali leaned over him. "Don't rip that paper."

"I'll try not to," he replied as he pushed on the top, attempting to compact it a little to see if he could gently push it back into the trunk and somehow get it out from a different angle without ripping it open.

Trying to help, Ali leaned in closer and freed the edge of the bow from underneath the latch. When she did, her hip brushed his. It was a pleasant sensation. Jake held his ground and didn't step away. A strand of her incredible hair moved like silk over his arm when she reached inside the trunk, and the scent of her spicy perfume caught him by surprise. He hadn't smelled good perfume in almost a year, and he'd almost forgotten how pleasant the aroma could be. He wouldn't be forgetting this scent for a long time.

After a few minutes more of trying, he managed to get the box out. "It's free," he said, surprised at how heavy it was. "I'll carry it in the house for you."

"You don't have to. The deal was just to get it out of the trunk."

"I wouldn't think of letting you take this inside alone." He looked at her puzzled face. "A do-gooder always has to finish the job."

Ali shrugged. "Okay, then—go ahead and carry it if you insist."

Jake's smile grew. "Oh, you bet I do."

Ali walked next to Jake as he carried the drum set up the walk toward the front door. Shoulders back, head up, his stride was long and relaxed. She liked that. A walk like his exuded confidence. She also liked his hair. Dark, short, cropped close around his ears but slightly longer on top, it framed his oval face perfectly. He had a straight nose and dark blue eyes that seemed lit with amusement by the laid-back grin that made his lips seem much too enticing.

At the door, he stopped and held the box directly in front of him. He angled his head toward her and she turned and looked into his eyes. There she saw a mixture of delight and interest that made her wonder for a moment what he might be thinking.

But she had no time to contemplate the possibilities because the front door opened at that moment.

Nick looked from her to the box. "What have you got there?" he asked Ali.

She smiled. "Oh, that's a surprise."

"But it's not as much of a surprise as this one," she heard Jake say.

She turned in time to see him set the box down on the stoop, hold his arms out, and say "Surprise!"

"Jake, you're here!" Nick exclaimed as he threw his arms around his cousin and patted him on the back. "We didn't expect you for another couple of hours."

"I caught a ride instead of waiting for the bus," Jake explained.

Ali looked from Nick to Jake and then back to Nick again. "You two know each other?"

"He's my cousin," Nick said. "We haven't seen him for over a year." He glanced at Ali. "But I didn't know that you'd met him."

Ali's head swiveled ever so slowly to Jake. "We just did," she said between clenched teeth.

Her narrow-eyed gaze caught Jake full force. When their eyes locked, Jake couldn't help but feel that if looks were laser beams, then his head would have exploded.

Chapter Three

Just like a twist on an old movie, her life imitated art right now. Of all the parties in all the universe, he had to be coming to this one. Ali grabbed a handful of potato chips from a bowl on the food table set up in the backyard and found a space for them on her plate. It was pure comfort food. She could eat about ten bags of chips right now to mollify the awkwardness she felt.

She found an empty chair near the pool and balanced the plate on her knees. She looked at the clear blue water, annoyed that her impulsive nature had gotten the best of her again. When on earth would she ever learn to think first, speak later? She probably never would, she decided. She was too much like her mother.

"I thought you were on a diet for the wedding," a voice from behind her said. Linda Wolff, her brother's fiancée, sat down on a chaise lounge next to her.

"Not today," Ali said, putting a healthy spoonful of potato salad into her mouth. "I'm probably going to eat everything in sight, so I hope my sister didn't plan on leftovers."

"It's only noon. How could you be having a bad day already?" Linda asked.

"How do you know it's a bad day?"

Linda gestured to her plate. "I always eat when I'm stressed. Looks like you do too."

Ali put the plate down on the flagstone pool deck. "You can't imagine what I did."

Linda laughed. "I saw the drum set."

"By the time I'm done adding to that drum set on birthdays, when Michael is twelve, he's going to have a whole percussion section. But that's not it," Ali replied with a swipe of her hand in the air.

Linda's smile grew wider. "This family is something else."

"Sure you want to marry into it?" Ali asked.

Linda glanced over at Trent. "Absolutely." Then she looked back at Ali. "But what's making you load up on carbs?"

"Jake Daultry," Ali replied with a sigh of exasperation.

"Do you mean Nick's cousin?"

Ali nodded.

"He just got here. What did he do?"

Linda looked positively perplexed. "It wasn't what he did. It was what *I* did," Ali explained. "I ran into him out front and ended up pouring out the family secrets to him."

"There aren't many secrets in the Archer family," Linda said.

"The ring thing," Ali confessed, shaking her head. "I blurted it out like I was some kind of head case." She saw Linda begin to grin. "Don't laugh," she warned. Her eyes cut to the pool. "I'll bet the water is cold this time of the year."

"I know you don't think that those rings really did anything."

"Normally I wouldn't," Ali agreed. "But Mom and I went shopping last week and she just gushed about the baby, and your wedding, and how I needed to play catch-up. Then, in a way only Tess Archer can, she commented on how it all seemed to start when she gave us Grandma Vicky's rings." She looked at her mother over Linda's shoulder.

This time Linda laughed. "It's only coincidence, Ali." She saw Jake come out of the house and head for the grill. She pointed to him. "But you have to admit, Jake Daultry is very attractive."

"Only if you like six-foot, solidly built guys with great eyes," Ali replied without thinking.

"So you did notice."

"Maybe a little."

"And when you did, the first thing out of your mouth was something about the rings." Linda tapped a finger on her lips. "Maybe you're under some sort of spell."

"Stop it!" Ali instructed. "He probably thinks I'm the person in the family that everyone pats on the head and says things like 'she's harmless enough' about."

"What did you say to him?"

"I think Jake thought I was proposing."

Linda shook her head. "I doubt it. There's not enough

time for a wedding. He's just here for thirty days and then he's going back to Iraq."

"He's a soldier?"

"And a darn fine one, I understand."

"Well, that explains the haircut and the duffel bag."

Linda tossed her head. "He's staring at you, Ali."

Ali glanced toward the house and caught Jake's gaze. The minute their eyes locked, she felt a shiver run down her spine. Brazenly male and utterly confident in its character, she saw his gaze run over her before he caught her eyes again and waved. She waggled her fingers at him in return and then turned her attention back to Linda.

"Is he gone?" Ali asked. Linda began to turn toward the house, but Ali reached out and grabbed her shoulder. "No, don't look at him."

"Then how am I going to find out if he's gone?" Linda asked.

"Okay, but be discreet."

But Linda was not about to buy into Ali's game. She spun on her heels, waved at Jake and then turned back. "Nope, he's still there and still staring at you."

"Thanks," Ali said, trying to make herself as small as possible on the outdoor chair. "Remind me never to ask you to be a spy."

"Your sister seems nice," Jake said as he walked to the grill, open hot dog bun on his plate.

"Who—you mean Mooch? I suppose if you're not on her B-list she's nice enough," Trent replied, glancing over at Ali.

Jake smiled at the brotherly barb. "You call her Mooch?"

"It's a family thing. Her real name is Allamuchy."

Jake raised his eyebrows. "That's different."

"I won't bore you with an explanation. Nick said you only have a thirty-day leave, and explaining the Archers can take years." Trent flipped some of the burgers. "So you're a career soldier, I hear."

Jake nodded.

"And you're going back to Iraq."

Jake nodded again.

"Why?"

"I could try to tell you, but explaining that to a civilian could also take years. Let's just say I'd like to help finish something the squad started over there."

"Fair enough," Trent said, basting a steak with barbeque sauce.

"It's not all bad, you know," Jake defended. "There are a lot of good things happening that the media doesn't bother to report."

Trent looked at the fire in Jake's eyes and held up his hands, potholder on one, spatula in the other. "Don't go all red-white-and-blue on me now. I know there are three sides to every story: one side, the other side, and the truth which usually lies somewhere in the middle. I don't judge. I just hope everything works out."

Jake pressed his lips together. "Sorry, sometimes I get a little carried away." Jake glanced at Ali, who caught his gaze. "So, let's get back to Ali then," he said as he waved to her. "What's she like?"

"You interested in my sister?" Trent asked with a grin on his face.

"We met out front and talked for a few minutes. She seemed nice enough, that's all." Jake hoped his voice didn't scream "liar." Truth was, he was interested in Ali. She had piqued his interest big time.

"For as much as I try to torture her whenever possible, truth is, Mooch is the best," Trent confessed. "She's always been there for me, loyal as all get-out, and honest as the day is long. But with that comes outspokenness. She speaks her mind and will tell you just how it is. You never have to wonder what she's thinking. Wait five minutes and she'll tell you."

"I think I may have run into the outspoken part of her outside," Jake said with a smile. He looked in her direction again. The sun had just come out from behind the clouds and seemed to have painted gold sparkle into that mane of red he found so fascinating to watch.

"Want me to call her over?" Trent offered.

"No, I can handle it."

Trent whistled. "Then I hope you have your body armor on, because even from this distance, I can tell by the look on her face that something's up." He tossed his head in Ali's direction. "She's talking to Linda, my fiancée, and I'll bet you a ten-spot that she's telling Linda about something I did to her when we were kids, just to get even with me." He put the burgers that were done on a plate as he spoke. "She thinks I got engaged just to irritate her."

"Does she really think that—that you'd propose marriage to your girlfriend just to irritate her?"

"Well, not just to irritate her." Trent unwrapped a few more burgers and placed them on the grill grates. "Remember I told you it would take years to explain?" When Jake nodded, Trent continued. "Mooch thinks that mom put some sort of love curse on the family using Grandma Vicky's rings and that Somer and I fell prey to it. Mooch thinks she's next, and she doesn't like it one bit."

"She said something about that out in the driveway."

Trent didn't look all that surprised. "That's Mooch. Speak first, and find out what you've said later. I think the whole thing has her spooked. You'd better be careful around her. I don't think she's taking any chances."

Jake laughed. "I'm back in the States to get some R and R, not to get married, so I think I'm safe."

"But, if you don't mind, I will be teasing her about this every chance I get."

"I suppose siblings do that to each other all the time."

"You don't have any?" Trent asked as he speared a well-done hot dog and set it on the bun on Jake's plate.

"Hit me with some fried onions too," Jake said, as he pried the hot dog bun open wider. "No, we Daultrys seem to come in singles. The best we can do is enjoy our cousins."

Ali's cell phone pinged its announcement of a text message. She took it out of the pocket of her jeans and noticed it was from Somer. That was odd, she thought. Without bothering to read it, she searched out her sister and found her in the kitchen cleaning some serving trays.

"What's up, sis?" she asked.

Somer dunked a dirty plate into a sink filled with sudsy

water. "Nothing, what's up with you?" Somer replied, scrubbing some sauce from it.

Ali picked up a dishtowel and began to dry some of the dishes Somer had already washed. "You texted me, so I thought I'd come and see in person what you needed."

Somer shook her head. "That text didn't come from me. I've been in here up to my elbows in dish soap."

Ali put down the towel and took the phone out of her pocket again. She angled it to her sister. "Then some-one is using your phone."

Somer glanced at the screen. "It seems so."

Ali looked around the room and then out the window. Everyone seemed busy enough. Her curiosity piqued as she pressed *View Now.*

The message said *"I like it when you smile."*

Somer tried to look at it. "What did I say?"

Ali pressed the phone to her chest. "You said I am the most amazing person you ever met, and you will worship me forever."

"I doubt that," Somer said, flicking soap bubbles at her sister. "Are you going to answer it?"

"Maybe," Ali replied, dramatically backing out of the room.

"Are you going to let me know what happens?" Somer called out.

Ali popped her head back around the corner. "That depends."

"On what?"

"It depends on whether I decide I like who you gave your phone to."

Chapter Four

Another text message popped up as Ali made her way to the front yard. *"Where did U go?"*

Ali sat down on the top step of the porch and answered back. *"U R not my sister, so who wants to know?"* She sent the message and stared at the phone, waiting.

"Guess" came the return text.

Ali typed her answer quickly. *"If I have to, I'll say Jake."* She pressed SEND and smiled.

"Why him?" was the next message.

"IDK, maybe because he wants to apologize for setting me up" she replied.

"And not because U think he's charming and good-looking?" followed the ping of the reply.

"HARDLY" she typed, knowing that all caps would get her point across, although she had to admit, Jake was both. *"Well, maybe a little of both"* she quickly sent before waiting for a return note.

"Good" came the one-word reply.

Ali smiled, enjoying the game. *"So where are U?"* she keyed back.

"Look to the right" was the immediate reply.

Ali swiveled her head and saw Jake standing at the edge of the house holding the cell phone in the air. "You may as well join me," she called to him. "Somer may have to pay per text message, and you're running up her bill."

"I'll leave her a twenty," he said, walking toward her. When he was right in front of her, he slipped the cell phone into his pants pocket.

"You're crazy," Ali said to him, giving him an accusing stare. She saw the crow's feet around his eyes deepen when he smiled.

"I've been known to do much crazier things." He gestured to the step. "Mind if I join you?"

Ali tossed her head and slid over. "Be my guest."

She took a moment to study him as he sat. Jake Daultry—it was a nice name, and he had a nice sense of humor. Laugh lines edged his mouth, and the corners lifted naturally, accenting the amusement in his cobalt-colored eyes. Nick hadn't mentioned much about him. She wondered why.

"I guess I should apologize for setting you up," Jake said. "I really should have introduced myself when I walked up to you. I guessed you were going to the same place I was headed when I saw you struggling with the box in your trunk. I just wanted to see what might happen."

She shook her head. "Whatever possessed you to do

that, anyway? Didn't you think it might be a bit uncomfortable once we got inside?"

Jake shrugged, grinning. "I didn't mean to, but when you spun around and confronted me, you looked like you courted adventure, so I wanted to see what would happen if I played along."

"And what happened?" she challenged.

The amusement in Jake's eyes flared. "Nothing's happened yet, but it's still early." He straightened and extended his hand. "Let's start over." He held her eyes with his gaze. "My name's Jake—Jake Daultry, Nick's first cousin."

His hand was warm and firm when Ali took it, returning his devastating smile at the same time. "Hi, I'm Ali Archer, Somer's sister."

"There," Jake said, letting go of her hand and leaning back on the porch railing with his elbows. "Now that the formalities are out of the way, we can relax."

"And do what?" Ali asked.

"How about we get to know each other?"

Ali grimaced. "I think you know a little too much about me already."

Jake's smile turned into a laugh. "You mean the family thing."

"I should apologize to you for that one. I think you thought I wanted to elope."

Jake shook his head. "I don't have time even to do that, I'm afraid."

Ali scooted back and mimicked his pose. "You're not into adventure, huh?" She reacted immediately to the wary look on his face. "I'm not meaning to pry or anything."

"I didn't think you were."

"Good," Ali said, "because I'm not."

Jake cocked his head. "This ring thing really has gotten to you, hasn't it?"

"No," she said quickly, then sighed. "Maybe it has a little. At this point, I'm not taking anything for granted." She straightened and scanned the area. "She didn't send you out here, did she?"

Raising his brows, Jake asked, "Who?"

"My mother, Tess Archer—she didn't send you over to me, right?"

Jake shook his head. "I just met her a few minutes ago, and we really didn't talk much. Getting through everyone at this party could take days. It seems as though the whole state is here."

Ali nodded. "I know. That's my sister. Go big or go home. You should have seen her wedding."

"You've segued to marriage again," Jake warned.

Ali smacked her forehead with the palm of her hand. "What is wrong with me?" She turned to Jake. "Run—escape now while you can."

"I'll take my chances," Jake replied.

"Okay then," Ali conceded, "but you can't say I didn't try to warn you."

Jake laughed. "Do you live in Westfield too?"

"No, I have a town house in Hillsborough. It's close to my job."

"And what is that?"

"I work for Somerset County."

"Ah, so you're one of those government workers I hear so much about."

Ali nodded. "Yes I am."

"What do you do?"

"I'm in the Environmental Section. I'm the Recycling Coordinator to be exact."

"Now that's what I call jumping on the 'Go-Green' bandwagon," Jake teased.

"Hey, it's important," Ali countered. "And you're in the military. Does that mean you're on the shooting-at-people bandwagon?"

He chuckled. "Point taken. Actually, I'm usually the one getting shot at. I fly Black Hawk helicopters."

"Oh—so you're getting shot at *and* burning a hole in the ozone layer with your little flying machine. Doesn't the military realize how much damage those copters do to the environment? They guzzle so much precious fuel and spew so many toxins into the air."

"Hey, when I'm not flying, I make sure I separate bottles from cans and stack my newspapers in those special bins. Does that count?" he asked her.

"Thank you for doing your part, even if Uncle Sam isn't doing his." Ali primly responded. "Those plastic bottles get turned into useful things like Frisbees and park benches."

"So then you admit that I am helping."

She had walked into his trap—willingly. She laughed. "Okay, you got me."

"And no one else has yet?" Jake asked with a grin.

Ali cocked her head. "I don't have a significant other, if that's what you want to know."

"I guess it's my lucky day then, because neither do I."

"Are you sure my mother didn't send you out here?" Ali asked.

"I'm just a guy who likes to enjoy the moment."

"And nothing else?" Ali pressed, cautious of the attraction that was welling up inside her. The charisma surrounding Jake was hard to ignore. She peeked at his left hand and saw there was no hint of a ring. Although she wasn't looking for a man, for some reason she was relieved that he wasn't married. But she had to wonder if he had been. Someone as handsome and as charming as Jake couldn't possibly have remained single for long. "You're totally innocent?"

Laughing Jake held up his hand. "Maybe not totally, but I have no interest right at the moment in eloping— honest." He winked. "Even though the potential elopee is pretty darn cute."

Ali let out a short breath of air. "That's good. Well then, you texted me, so as the textee, I should be able to interrogate you at length and find out all about you without having to answer any of your questions. Agreed?"

Jake shook his head. "Not fair."

"How about if we take turns then?" Ali suggested.

"I'm flexible. Let's try it."

Ali slid her elbows back onto the top step and relaxed. "I'll go first. I'm a workaholic by nature. I'm making it my mission to try to educate everyone in the county about the benefits of going green. Right now I'm working on a program for the schools to introduce grade school kids to the benefits of recycling."

"How is that going?"

"Pretty well." She turned to him and her breath almost caught. The setting sun glinted behind him, outlining him in light and making him look almost angelic. "Your turn," she whispered. "How long have you been in the military?"

"I've been involved with it one way or another almost from the minute I was born, I think. I played soldiers from about the time I could walk, was Junior ROTC in high school, then went to West Point—so I guess that makes it all my life, basically. I love flying. I couldn't imagine doing anything else." Jake looked up, studying the deepening colors of the sky. "It's incredible up there. Sometimes, when the conditions are just right, you can feel like you're all alone and flying like Icarus did in the ancient myth. You're all alone and you're flying the sky."

Ali watched the fascination run across his features and knew he meant every word he'd said. Jake seemed different from most guys she knew—more centered, more sure of himself. It must be his military background, she concluded. The urge to know more about him filled every cell in her body.

"You seem really engrossed with flying."

"I love it. It's my job."

"What made you pick helicopters over planes, though?" she asked. "It seems to me that you're more the fighter-pilot type—you know, streaking across the sky miles up and making those weird white puffy lines in a clear blue sky."

Jake shrugged. "There was an opening that needed to

be filled, so I volunteered." He sat forward and leaned his forearms on his thighs. "I do what has to be done. I'm Army, a career man." He waited for a reaction. None came, so he went on. "I'm on a thirty-day leave now. This is actually my first full day back in the States."

Ali rolled her eyes. "And you land here. What are the odds?"

Jake tossed his head. "It's not bad so far."

"That's because you had the good sense to come out front with me."

"It could also be that ladies with red hair have always fascinated me."

Ali smiled and leaned closer to him. "I'll tell you a little secret." She tugged on a copper-colored ringlet. "It's not real."

Jake moved so his face was about two inches from hers. "It doesn't matter. I like the combination of gold, copper and red. It shows you have a lot of facets to your personality." As Ali's smile widened, the urge to kiss her revved through Jake like someone had rammed a foot on an accelerator positioned right in the middle of his chest.

His gaze roamed slowly over her face and settled on her lips. "You know, I haven't kissed a woman for a while," he said, his gaze never leaving her mouth.

"Is that right?" Ali replied.

"Uh-huh, that's right." He watched her press her lips together to moisten them a little. When they parted again, the rhythm of his heart ramped up to what a doctor would call tachycardia.

"Is there a prize or something for being the first

woman a soldier kisses when he comes back home?" she asked.

"Just the knowledge that you are serving your country, ma'am," Jake answered her.

"Never let it be said that an Archer wasn't patriotic."

Ali saw the intensity in Jake's eyes change right before she closed the distance between them and touched her lips to his. The contact was so galvanizing that she felt the breath catch in her throat. The moment was amazing.

She felt his moist breath on her cheek when he broke contact for the barest part of a second and said, "Do you think we should be making out on your sister's front steps?"

The scrape of his emerging beard on her cheek sent a delightful arc of prickles through her. "We're not 'making out' in the strictest sense of the phrase. I'm serving my country," she said right before she put her hands on his cheeks and found his lips again with hers.

There was strength in his kiss this time, but also an incredible gentleness when he molded his mouth to hers. A weightlessness flowed through her when he moved his head slowly, bringing her a sensation of pleasure that was pure and honest because he was sharing and not taking as a lot of men did.

Jake's kiss did not disappoint, even when he moved his lips to her cheek, to her nose, and then back to her lips again. She could taste a saltiness that intrigued her, and she inhaled his masculine scent as the kisses continued. She clasped her hand across his neck and held on for dear life.

Kathryn Quick

Gradually, Jake broke contact with her. As Ali let her hands glide down the sides of his face, their breaths mingled. He nuzzled her hair and kissed her quickly one more time before pulling back completely.

He stared at her for a few seconds, the smile on his face one of both wonder and amazement. Then he kissed her nose in a playful gesture and whispered, "God bless America."

Chapter Five

Ali stood and crossed her hands over her chest. "I have to admit, that was pretty slick."

Jake rose and faced her. He put his hands on her hips. "I have no idea what you mean," he countered, the amusement in his voice belying the seriousness he tried to project.

"I'm pretty sure you didn't learn that maneuver at West Point."

Jake just dipped his head, not confirming or denying Ali's comment.

She cocked her hips but didn't step back. She rested her right forearm on his left shoulder, her hand dangling over his back. "Haven't kissed a woman in a while?" Sarcasm layered her voice. "I seriously doubt it. How many have fallen for that line?"

"Do you mean besides you?"

Ali felt heat warm her cheeks. She'd fallen for it, all right. And she was not one bit sorry that she had. Her heart still pounded erratically in her chest, and she could gladly drown in brilliant blue of his hooded eyes. *Come up with something snappy to say,* she told herself. But all words refused to form when she saw him give her a very male smile. *Focus,* she heard her mind say, *and tell him something.*

"I just let you *think* I was falling for your line," she said, lifting her chin. *Oh yeah, that put him in his place.*

"And why would you do that?"

"I wanted to prove to you it wouldn't work." Ali felt her inner self roll her inner eyes. *When you're in a hole, stop digging,* her mind warned. She opened her mouth to counter, but ran into a situation much worse: her mother

"Ali and Jake, look at the two of you."

Ali peeked over Jake's shoulder. She could only imagine how it looked from Tess' vantage point. They appeared very intimate, she guessed, what with Jake's hand on her hips and her arm slung casually over his shoulder. There was no way her mother would believe she was trying to give Jake a lecture.

She stepped out of Jake's light hold. "Just talking, Mom."

Tess was beside them now. She looked from Jake's satisfied grin to Ali's guilty one. "I'm sure, dear. Do you think you can stop long enough to join us all for dessert? Somer's about to bring out cake and coffee."

"That would be fine, ma'am," Jake said.

Tess turned fully to him and put her hand on his arm. "We don't stand on formalities in the Archer family. Please call me Tess."

"Yes, ma'am." When Tess raised her finger in reprimand, Jake nodded. "I mean Tess."

"It's not often I meet a real hero," Tess said, beaming. "I mean, we see them on the news, but to meet someone in person is a whole lot more meaningful for me."

"I'm not a hero, ma'am, just a soldier doing my job."

Tess looked from Jake to Ali and shot her daughter her sweetest smile. "Jake, you're going have to practice saying my name. It's Tess," she corrected, turning her attention back to him.

"I'll have to do that," he returned.

Ali grabbed Jake's arm and pulled him away from her mother. "Mom, we'll be inside in a minute."

"Certainly, dear—but don't be long. I think your sister wants you to explain to the whole family about the drum set."

"I'll explain it all to Michael about this time next year when he's walking. That'll be more fun," Ali said as her mother walked away.

"Stop it!" Ali nearly shouted to Jake when her mother turned the corner of the house.

"Stop what?"

Ali waved her hands in front of her. "Stop being all charming and stuff. My mother loves that."

"My mom told me to always be polite."

"Be polite, yes. But I suggest you dial down the charm a notch, fly-boy, or she'll go into yenta mode, and then you're toast. Look what happened to my sister and my brother."

Jake grinned. "Do you think I'm charming?"

Ali glared. "You know you are."

"Okay, Maybe I am—a little."

"For your own good, try not being all 'golly gee ma'am, shucks, I'm just a country boy' around her."

"But I'm not at all country. I was born in Hoboken," he cut in.

Her eyes flared. "You are driving me crazy."

He almost laughed out loud. "Right back at you."

"Don't you understand that I am trying to save your camouflaged hide?"

"By screaming at me?"

"No, I'm trying to save you by telling you that if you keep up this nice-guy routine, you're going to fall right into her trap."

"I think you've already fallen into that trap, Ali."

She began to open her mouth, but then realized he just might be right and stopped. She began to pace and talk at the same time. "Oh, she's a smart one." She walked to him. "And I bet my sister and my brother are both in on it."

Jake took a step back and just watched her pace. Ali Archer—he liked her, redheaded spitfire that she was and all. Could he help it that her beautiful eyes invited him to join her in whatever adventure she was having at the time, or that that hair of hers reminded him of a vivid sunset over the desert? Now that he'd made that connection, he knew that he would never fly another mission in the sand again without thinking of her.

"So we're agreed then," he heard her say as she stalked off in the direction of the side yard. "We're not going to encourage anything for the rest of the party here."

"Let's just see what develops," he said as he followed her. She sure could walk fast when she wanted, he noted as he took a few seconds to catch up to her. "Ali, wait."

She didn't turn around, just held up a hand in his direction.

In another stride he was next to her. "You and I know there's nothing happening here, so let's relax and enjoy the rest of the party."

She stopped and faced him. "You're right. You must think I'm one big fool."

He shook his head. "No, I don't. Family dynamics are complicated, I hear."

Ali sighed. "Some are more complicated than others." She crossed her arms over her chest and looked down at the grass. "This is insane." She looked at him. "You should be having fun, not listening to a crazy woman carry on like I did."

"I am having fun," Jake assured her.

Ali snorted and then covered her mouth with her hand. "Sorry, I know that wasn't very ladylike." She stepped back so she could focus on his face. "Maybe once you get away from my over-enthusiastic family, you can relax and enjoy your leave."

"I don't mind at all. Since I met you, it's been interesting to say the least." He saw a blush fill her cheeks.

"Are you being polite or charming now?"

"Neither. I mean it."

She let out a small sigh. "I have to admit, you are definitely interesting, Jake Daultry."

"So I've made a good first impression, at least."

She nodded. "You've made an impression, all right."

"It's all right as long as I'm memorable," he quipped in return.

"I'll remember you, no doubt about that."

The amusement she saw fill his eyes made her laugh. He did make an impression on her. His being fun, relaxed, and downright handsome, that's what she would remember about him after the party was over.

And there was something else, something unexpected. She'd remember the strong, undeniable urge to lean forward and kiss him that seemed to simmer inside her whenever she looked into his incredible eyes. Maybe it was all her fault; the combination of her nephew's party, her brother's engagement, and thinking about her grandmother's citrine ring made her want to find herself in Jake's embrace again.

But the feeling of his arms around her had been nice—warm, strong, and, if she dared admit it, a tiny bit masterful . . . as was his kiss. Could you blame a girl for wanting to sample it all again before he went on his way, probably never to cross paths with her again except at family gatherings at her sister's house?

His playful smile made her slide her hands onto his shoulders. She would have the last move in the chess game.

"Thirty days of freedom, huh?"

He rested his hands on her hips, countering her move. "I have a month to be just me."

She trailed her finger down his cheek. "G.I. Joe goes civvy. This could be interesting."

He turned his head and kissed the tip of her finger. "Depends."

She saw his eyes light with anticipation as he waited to see what she would do next. "It depends on what?" she baited. Ali found herself drawn into the smoky blue of his eyes. She wondered briefly if she hadn't gone a bit too far and backed herself into a corner. But the gentle massage of his fingers on her hip banished the fear almost as quickly as it came.

"Well, I'd say it depends on if you'd be willing to spend some of those thirty days with me," Jake answered.

Ali meant to tell him that she didn't think that was possible, but instead surrendered to the promise in Jake's tender gaze, a promise of both adventure and tenderness. Her lashes swept downward and her lips parted slightly, waiting for contact with his strong mouth.

Jake Daultry did not make her wait long.

This time his kiss was powerful when his lips touched hers. There was nothing tentative or simple in the way he possessed her mouth like a man on a mission. Ali met and matched his heated quest, lost in a series of molten, heated explosions that rocked through her.

His hands moved to her back, and she tilted her head back more, feeling him trail tiny kisses down the length of her throat. She had no idea what this man had done to get to her so quickly and so completely, but somehow he felt right. She homed in on the warmth of his hands on her back and the soft trail of fire his kisses left along her jaw before he returned to her lips.

A small sound, a breathless sigh escaped her. Her fingers alternately opened and closed against his chest, and she could feel the pounding of his heart racing in time with hers. Unaccustomed to reacting like this to any man's kiss, Ali tried to stop herself from falling through the vortex of heat that spiraled through her, making her dizzy and forcing her to lose the last shred of common sense she was trying to hold on to with all she had. She ran her hands from his shoulders to the sides of his face and gently pulled in closer.

Help came in the form of her brother's voice. "Mooch, Mom would be proud!"

Slowly she drew away from Jake's wonderfully pliant lips. She was sure her face was flushed and that if she opened her eyes, the drowsiness of enjoyment would be a dead giveaway. "Seems I've developed a weakness for the military," she whispered to Jake, watching her brother stride to them out of the corner of her eye.

"You're pretty heady stuff yourself, for a civilian," Jake replied.

"Now, boys and girls," Trent said, shouldering himself between Ali and Jake, "we wouldn't want Mom to get her hopes up, now would we?"

Ali ducked out from under the arm Trent threw over her shoulder. "We were just coming to join you all."

"That's not how it looked from where I stood," Trent corrected.

"And as usual, you only saw half of what happened," Ali warned him.

"And you didn't have to yell out 'smooch' and call attention to us," Jake defended, trying to help. "That's not what was happening." He wasn't lying, he reasoned. You smooched your mother or your cousin or your maiden aunt, not a red-haired hottie who made your blood boil; you kissed her.

"You must have lip-lock on the brain, Daultry. I was calling my sister. Remember I told you her nickname?"

Jake pulled down his brows. "I forgot, I guess."

"That's because my sister was giving you mouth-to-mouth, but she was doing it all wrong." He spun to face Ali. "Sister dear, you're supposed to pinch his nose with your fingers, not cover his ears with your hands."

"Jake was breathing just fine!" Ali protested.

"Do tell," Trent pressed.

She shot her brother a warning look, grabbed one of Jake's hands, and pulled him toward the backyard.

Just before she turned the corner to the backyard, she looked back at her bother, who was laughing so hard he had to wrap his arms around his stomach to try to catch his breath.

"He is so dead," Ali mumbled as she turned the corner and walked right into Linda.

She did quick introductions. "Linda Wolff, meet Jake Daultry." They nodded to each other. "Linda is my brother's fiancée," she added in explanation.

"Where is Trent?" Linda asked. "I was just going to look for him."

"He's around the side doing his best imitation of the Village Idiot." Ali pointed behind her. "Are you sure you want to marry him?"

Linda put a hand on her hip. "What did he do to you this time?"

"Tell you what," Ali replied, "you get his version,

guaranteed to only be able to be described as sci-fi fantasy, and then come find me. I'll tell you the truth."

As Linda walked away, Ali and Jake heard her mumble something like "Archers—once you fall in love with one, you know you'll never leave him, but every now and then, you sure are darn tempted to leave him by the side of the road for a few days."

Chapter Six

Ali and Jake had only taken a step into the backyard when a volleyball hit Jake in the leg.

"Here, dude," one of the kids who was lined up on the far side of the net called out.

Jake picked up the ball and tossed it to him. The kid caught it and promptly served it to the other side. There was no return, only some rousing laughs as the ball flew all the way back to the edge of the fence about thirty yards back.

"Hardly seems fair," Jake commented as he watched a little girl of about ten run to retrieve it.

Ali glanced over at the two teams lined up. Jake was right. It seemed like all the teenagers were on one side of the net and the younger kids on the other. She did a quick head count and noted that the younger kids outnumbered the older kids by about five, but it didn't seem to matter as the older kids continued to serve the ball way over the heads of the younger ones.

"Maybe we should do something to even out the odds."

"Ali, Jake," she heard her mother call out, "come and get a piece of your nephew's cake."

Ali looked over and saw her mother waving to them, spatula in her hand. There would be no escape.

"Are you ready for interrogation, soldier?" she asked Jake.

He looked from the volleyball game to Tess. "She looks harmless enough."

Ali feigned shock. "Did they teach you nothing in basic training? The innocent-looking ones are the ones you have to be particularly careful around." She leaned back on her right leg and crossed her arms over her chest. "Look closely at her. Look at that big smile she's wearing as she cuts the cake into big chunks to make sure everyone gets a big piece."

"There's nothing unusual about that. I think it's a mother thing."

Ali shook her head. "Uh-uh, you don't understand. It's all part of her plan. Those pieces covered in white frosting will gives us a huge sugar rush. Then in an hour or so, when our metabolism crashes, she'll have us right where she wants us. That's when she'll put her plan into action." She leaned forward and whispered, "If you know what's good for you, you'll stay away from the cake."

Jake laughed. "She's not a terrorist, Ali."

Ali looked up at him. "Oh, really? I know how she operates. Once she gets you into a big, fat carb coma, she'll start with a thousand questions, and then, bam!" She reached out and smacked his arm with her palm. "You're part of the family and she's introducing you to some third cousin I can't remember we even had who just lost a hundred pounds."

Jake's shoulder shook as he laughed. "I doubt that's going to happen."

"Oh disbeliever, I've seen her in action. Do not eat the cake."

Tess looked up from the cake plate as if on cue. She waved the cake cutter in the air. "It's almost gone. Hurry over, you two."

They began to walk to the table when the volleyball came at them again. "No fair," they heard one of the younger children say. "You guys hit it too hard."

Jake threw the ball back and watched for a few minutes as the lopsided game continued. What the boy said was true. The older kids weren't playing all that fair.

"You go on without me, Ali," he said. "I have to fix this."

She watched him jog over to the net and signal to the teams to gather around. The younger kids came first, but he had to have a little talk with the teens in order to coax them to the net. After a few minutes of talking, he waved Ali over.

"I need your help," he said to her. "We're about to make the teams a bit more even, and we need one more bigger kid."

Ali put her forefinger on her chest. "Bigger kid . . . meaning me?"

Jake nodded. "You'll be one captain, and I'll be the other." He tossed her the volleyball before she could refuse. "And we're picking sides. You can go first."

Ali thought she could sense what he wanted her to do. She choose the smallest player on the team. Jake did the same. They alternated choices until they had selected everyone around the net and the teams were much more even. When the last pick was made Jake winked at her and took his side with his team.

"But we're serving first," he called out, walking to the back line and picking up a little girl in blue shorts.

He brought her to the front line and held out the volleyball. Then he whispered in her ear. Her face brightened as she made a fist and hit the ball with all her might. Jake aided in delivering the serve by making sure the ball got airborne by tossing it in Ali's direction. Soon the game was underway with the teens taking their cue from Jake. They helped the younger kids with their serves and made sure the ball was returned so it could be hit back.

After that it became more play than game as the teens eventually found it was more fun to include the younger kids than to try to show them up. They began to show the kids how to serve and hit and play. Soon everyone was laughing and having fun.

Ali and Jake took their cues and left the game. "What did you promise the bigger kids?" Ali asked as they finally made their way to the dessert table.

"What makes you think I promised them anything?"

Ali scoffed. "They gave in awfully easily. Besides, when I was a little kid, my brother was a teenager. He made it his life's work, until he was about seventeen and found a steady girlfriend, to make sure I was properly humiliated every day."

Jake laughed. "I didn't promise them anything. I just asked them if they were really having fun playing kids who couldn't give them a real run in the game. After they thought about it for a while, they admitted it had been fun for a while, but not so much as the game went on."

Ali nodded her approval. "I guess they did teach you some tactical maneuvers in the Army, after all."

Jake arched his arm around Ali's shoulders. "If you want, I can show you some real tactical maneuvers later on." He waggled his eyebrows up and down.

Ali ducked out of his hold. She glanced at her mother, who was watching their every move. "Well, that sounds potentially interesting, but not here and not now. I believe we're late for cake."

The clear night allowed all the stars to be out, it seemed, as Jake walked Ali down the driveway.

"It turned out to be a great party, after all," Ali admitted as they reached her car. She leaned back onto the front fender.

"Yes it did," Jake agreed, facing her, legs spread, hands in the back pocket of his jeans. "I think you had a lot to do with that."

Ali brushed off his comment with a swipe of her hand. "Nah, I don't think so. I'm just happy you survived it." She looked down at the ground and then back up into his eyes. "So, you're going home now."

He nodded.

Ali struggled with what to say next. He interested her. She wanted to know more about him and wasn't quite ready to come to terms with not seeing him at least one more time. Maybe she could lead him into asking her out.

"Any plans for the rest of your leave?" she asked.

"Not really—I just want to enjoy being stateside before I get back to the sand."

"I guess that means you won't be visiting the New Jersey shore before you go?"

"Not if I can help it," he replied. "I'm still picking sand out of body parts."

Ali covered her eyes. "Oh, that is totally TMI." She looked back at him. "Is there anything you really *have* to do before you go back? I mean, is there something that you promised yourself you would do or see?"

Jake seemed to contemplate her question before answering. "No, there's not, not really."

"What about a Broadway show, or a concert or a football game—you have plans for seeing one of those?"

He shook his head.

"Do you have any plans to play tennis, take a karate class, or go to a garage sale?"

"No, I have plans for none of them. Why do you ask?"

Ali widened her eyes. "I ask because I'm trying to get you to beg to see me again, and I'm running out of ideas."

Jake grinned, the smile lighting his eyes more than the lamppost next to them lit the street. "I want to, but I didn't want to be pushy."

"You have only thirty days, soldier. You'd better push a little."

"How's dinner Friday night?"

"Do you mean the Friday that's five whole days away?"

He took a step closer to her. "How does Wednesday sound, then?"

"Better."

"I'll call you tomorrow to let you know where."

She took a step closer to him and erased the rest of the distance between them. "One condition, though."

Jake put his hands on her shoulders. His forefingers gently caressed the sides of her neck. "And what would that be?"

"You can never tell my mother," Ali said just before she rose up on her toes and kissed him.

Chapter Seven

The first voice Ali heard when she walked to the elevator of the parking deck at the county administration building the next day was that of her co-worker Diana.

"How'd the drum set go over?" Diana asked with a laugh.

Ali pushed the DOWN button once she got to the elevator pod. "With a bang," she smirked.

"Your thoughtful gift was much appreciated?"

"My sister and the hub, not so much, but the rest of the family got a kick out of it." Ali moved to her right to make room for a few other county employees.

"So the party wasn't as much of a drudge as you thought it was going to be?" Diana asked.

"No, that turned out not to be so much of a problem."

"The way you were talking about it all week, I expected you to come in here with a cast on your leg from being dragged out of your car and into the house."

"Tell you later," Ali said as the elevators doors opened and they stepped inside with about four other people.

Not sure she wanted to share her weekend with the whole county, as she would if the gossip mill was in gear, Ali leaned against the back of the elevator car.

Diana's mention of the weekend brought Jake Daultry to the forefront of her mind—not that anyone had to mention him in order for her to think about him. Jake was a man of many faces. Mostly he'd been the quiet and restrained type when there were a lot of people around, she noticed as she had watched him for the rest of the party. She guessed that had come from his stint in Iraq. Paying attention, watching—it must be ingrained in him from that.

But there were times that, through the hard shell of the soldier he had to be, some of the softer side of Jake Daultry came out, and not just during the time he spent alone with her. She had to admit, she had let him pull her into his little trap and let him kiss her. It hadn't been much of a trap anyway.

It was the interest he'd displayed in the neighborhood children during the backyard volleyball game that had surprised her. He'd noticed right away that most of the younger kids were on one team, and that the teens were giving them an old-fashioned volleyball shellacking. The look on his face and in his eyes when he'd seen how much fun the game had become for everyone after he'd intervened—but very coolly—made her want to know him better, even if it would only be for the rest of his leave.

At ground level, everyone exited the elevator. Diana waited until the crows thinned and then pressed Ali. "Something saved the weekend for you. Who was it?"

Ali stopped walking. "Why do you say it was a who?"

"Because we spent a few hours Googling diseases you could have to get you out of going, we almost got me to call and say you had to go into work, and generally, you never do anything you don't want to do, including stay somewhere you don't want to be. And, if I remember correctly, you were going to call me so we could go to an early movie." Diana looked at her watch. "You know, I'm still waiting for that call."

"Maybe there was someone who made it a bit more interesting," Ali grudgingly admitted. It had been a chance encounter. The man would be gone from the country in thirty days. How much harm could it do to admit he was cute and interesting?

They reached the first-floor elevator inside the building and joined a few other people there. The first car filled and Diana and Ali stayed behind.

"He was my brother-in-law's cousin on leave from Iraq," Ali finally admitted.

"Hmmm, that's interesting."

Ali knit her brow. "That's all I get, a 'that's interesting'?"

"Well, that's all I have to say so far. What else is there?"

"He's a helicopter pilot."

"So he's a fly-boy, and what else?"

"He's going back to Iraq at the end of the month."

"Okay, so he's returning to the war front in a few weeks, and what else?"

"He's nice."

Diana threw up her hands, her handbag rolling back

to her elbow. "Cut to the chase, girlfriend! What does he *look* like?"

Ali could feel her smile widen as she thought about Jake. "He's tall, with dark hair and blue eyes," she stopped.

"And what else about him is giving you that goofy smile?" Diana prompted.

"He's cute," Ali confirmed just as the doors on the second elevator door opened.

Ali sat at her desk in her cubicle in the County Planning Board Department on the third floor with the telephone cradled against her shoulder, listening to the canned music as she waited for the administrative assistant for the Sunnymead Elementary School principal to come back on the line.

Diana walked in with an armful of papers, and Ali pressed the speakerphone button, freeing her hand. She set the phone receiver back in the cradle.

"We still need to finish our conversation. You haven't told me any details," Diana pressed, holding the stack of papers out to Ali. "These are the newest recycling contracts for the municipalities. They need signatures."

"There's nothing to tell." Ali signaled to the corner of her desk and Diana set the contracts down.

"Are you going to see him again?"

"What for? You can't start anything meaningful in thirty days, and I'm not hopping on the adopt-a-soldier bandwagon just because of three degrees of separation. It wouldn't be honest."

"I didn't mean that," Diana said, sliding into the chair

next to Ali's desk. "I just thought it would be nice to help ease him into civilian life for a few days."

Jake's face flashed through Ali's mind, underscoring what she thought about him when she'd met him. "Diana, no one who looks that good doesn't have someone waiting to help him do just that. I'm not getting in the way, or filling a spot for a few weeks."

"He's really that good-looking?"

Ali nodded. "I know I'd be tempted if I was sure he wasn't attached."

"Do you know for sure either way?"

Just then the principal's secretary came on the speakerphone and one of the administrative assistants in Ali's department tapped on the wall of her cubicle. Ali grabbed the phone and held up her finger in a sign that meant "wait." As Ali confirmed her appointment with the school, Diana took the pink message slip from the assistant's hand.

"Okay, where were we?" Ali asked when she hung up the phone.

Diana handed her the message. "You were about to tell me more about G.I. Joe."

"Great," Ali said, dropping her chin, her voice clipped.

Diana sat back. "Whoa, did something I say just hit a nerve?"

"No," Ali said. "I just confirmed a presentation on recycling with the second-grade class of Sunnymead Elementary School for tomorrow at ten." She held up the message. "And Melissa just called in saying she has the flu, and her doctor has advised her to stay home for the rest of the week."

"She had better stay home," Diana agreed. "I'm going on vacation next week, and I don't need a disease."

Ali scowled. "The school's principal wants all the bells and whistles to keep the class's attention during the presentation." She pressed her lips together in a frown. "So you know what that means now that Melissa is out of service."

Diana burst out laughing. "Guess you're about to become Bundles, the recycling mascot, aren't you?"

The next day at close to 10:00 A.M., Ali walked down the tiled hall of Sunnymead Elementary School with a giant penguin head tucked under her arm. The black penguin suit was hotter than Hades and sort of smelled like the inside of a suitcase—or what she thought the inside of a suitcase might smell like.

Besides, once she became Bundles, the only way she could see out was through the mesh that made up part of the penguin's beak. Then the only viewing option was straight on, and it was hard enough to walk without running into walls or excited kids. It was especially tricky with kids who broke away from the aide taking them to the bathroom because they'd rather hold on to a big, soft penguin.

It wasn't that she didn't love children. But Bundles had flippers for hands, and it wasn't easy to peel off kids' hugs without opposable thumbs. Those little guys were stronger than they looked, especially when one's center of gravity suddenly dropped a foot due to costume design.

Her shoes were covered with orange feet, if you could

call them that. They were supposed to look like a penguin's, complete with painted-on claws, but they looked more like something Disney's Pluto would wear as he strolled through Tomorrowland in Florida. The only thing the oversized felt-covered shoe forms did was make a weird clomping sound when she walked.

Oh yes, Melissa owed her big time.

Ali maneuvered as best she could down the long hallway on her way to Ms. Fitzsimmon's second grade class, clomping along the tiled floor like a little girl trying on her mother's high heels. One left turn and she would be there. She'd decided to wait until she was right outside the door before she put on her head.

But then she turned the corner.

Down the hallway a bit, on one knee and in full dress uniform, holding a plastic helicopter high over his head with one hand and talking to a small boy looking up at the plane, was Jake Daultry. Ali stopped dead in her tracks. The picture took her breath away. She felt as though she was looking at a Norman Rockwell painting.

She started to step back in order not to break the moment, when she backed into a metal locker. The boy looked at her and shouted, "Hey, look—it's a big cat!"

That's when she had to presence of mind to jam the penguin head on. It was flippers-down just before Jake turned to look in her direction. She saw the boy come running at her full-speed and braced herself for impact. He hit her on a dead run and wrapped his arms around her at about hip level. If it wasn't for the lockers behind her, she would have ended up on the ground from the force of seven-year-old exuberance.

"Hi, cat," the boy called out, keeping her in his death grip.

Jake was about two steps behind him, helicopter still in hand. "Billy, I don't think that's a cat." He moved closer to Ali to get a better look. "What are you?" he asked her.

Ali didn't dare reply. There was no way Jake was going to know she was the one under all the felt. She tipped her head one way and then the other, trying to be as animated as possible without speaking.

About that time Jake noticed she couldn't move. "Billy, let the big"—he peered closer—"penguin, I think, go."

Billy complied. Ali took a step away from him and saluted her thanks with her right flipper.

But Billy wasn't done. He pulled on her left arm. "Where are you going?"

Ali looked at Jake through the mesh on her beak. He put his hand on Billy's shoulder, his body language telling her that he wasn't going anywhere until Billy got his answer. Ali raised a flipper and gestured down the hall.

"The kindergarten?" Billy asked.

Ali shrugged and waggled her head again. She attempted to step away from them but bumped her oversized shoe into the lockers. The tinny rattle brought two teachers out into the hall to see what had happened. Ali waved both flippers at them and, fortunately, they went back inside their classrooms.

She pointed as best she could down the hall and waved good-bye, hoping it would be enough.

It wasn't. Billy grabbed onto one flipper. "You could

come to my classroom too," he said. "I brought Mr. Daultry for show-and-tell, but Patty forgot hers, so you could be it." He turned to Jake. "You wouldn't mind sharing, would you?"

Jake grabbed Ali's other flipper. "No, I wouldn't mind that at all."

Trapped, Ali couldn't think as she was escorted to the last classroom door on the right. As Jake opened the door for Billy, she knew it was now or never.

"It's me, Ali," she said, her voice a bit muffled.

"Who?" Jake asked, trying to find an opening in the large head.

"Ali," she said again.

Jake appeared still to be unable to make out the word. "Why don't you go on inside, Billy?" He held out the toy helicopter. "Take this in and tell the class what I told you about flying it. I'll be inside in a second."

Billy nodded and bounced inside.

Jake turned to Ali. "Now, who did you say you were?"

Ali's shoulders slumped inside the suit. She reached up with her flippers and twisted off the head. "Ali," she said once the penguin head came off. "Couldn't you hear me?"

Jake became mesmerized when she shook her head to clear the hair from her eyes. She apparently had no idea what a striking picture she made when her hair danced around her face. Even in an oversized penguin suit, she looked great.

"Another of your talents?" he quipped as he watched a streak of pink grow across her cheeks.

"I do what I can," she replied.

He walked around her in a small circle. "So, in addition to saving the world for future generations, you're also a mascot of some sort."

She held up the head. "This is Bundles, the Recycling Penguin."

Jake's mouth formed a perfect O. "I get it. 'Bundles' as in how you should tie up things and put them in bins."

"Exactly—Bundles is very important to teaching schoolchildren about the benefits of recycling."

At about that time, the teacher poked her head out of the classroom. "Captain Daultry, the children are ready for you now." She looked at Ali. "And I think Ms. Fitzsimmon's class is waiting for you. Are you lost? Her class is two doors away." She pointed down the hall.

"Thanks," Ali replied.

"Captain Daultry, are you ready?" the teacher said.

"I'll be right in," he replied. When the door to the classroom closed, he turned to Ali. "Need some help getting your head on straight?"

"No," Ali replied, dragging out the word, "I'm capable." She turned to leave and bounced into the wall again.

"I can see that," Jake quipped.

"The regular person is out sick today. I don't do this all that much," she explained.

"How about I walk you to the classroom?"

Ali looked inside Billy's classroom. "No, the kids are waiting for you. You'd better get in there."

"How about if I call you later and we move our dinner date up to tonight?"

Ali was not about to leave anything to chance. "How

about I meet you in a hour in the playground and we talk about it there instead?"

Jake's face brightened. "That sounds like a plan. Which playground? I saw a couple on my way in."

"You've been trained by the United States Army to search and track. I'm sure you won't be able to miss me," she said. "I'll be the big stuffed animal sitting on a swing." In one fluid motion, Ali secured the penguin head over hers and walked down the hall.

Ali pushed back with the tip of her right shoe and set the swing into motion. After her talk to Ms. Fitzsimmon's second grade, she'd looked through the rectangular window of the classroom in which Jake was the object of Billy's show-and-tell.

Big mistake.

He stood tall and straight, hands clasped behind his back. She didn't know for sure, but from the small smile on his face, he appeared to be enjoying whatever it was one of the children in the class was telling him. Then a little girl's hand in the front row shot up, and he walked to her. She pointed to a paper on her desk and Jake dropped to one knee to get a better look.

That's when a current of warmth rushed through Ali and seemed to hit her heart. She gave her head a small shake wondering if this could be what it felt like to begin falling in love with someone, but rationalizing, in the next instant, that it was too soon for that.

First the volleyball game had gotten to her, and then the scene in the school hallway with Billy had taken her breath away. But neither was anything close to the joy and attention she'd seen on Jake's face as he'd listened to the small, ponytailed tot in the front row of the classroom.

Her conceptions of stiffly trained, military fighting men and all their hoo-wah programming were dashed completely when Jake took the paper from the little girl's hand and folded it before putting it into the inside pocket of his uniform jacket.

What on earth was she going to do now? The man had blown into her life like a military jet on recon, and he was about to blow back out of it in a short few weeks. She couldn't allow herself to develop feelings for someone like that. It would be too devastating to her heart.

Think, Ali, she scolded herself. There was a solution to the problem somewhere. She just had to find it.

She closed her eyes and tried to enjoy the slow rocking of the swing when she felt a pair of hands on her back, followed by a gentle push forward. She took hold of the silver chains that anchored the swing to its frame and looked back over her shoulder.

Jake was waiting for her to swing back to him.

"Hey," she said.

"Hey, yourself," he answered as she reached him on the backward movement and he gently gave her another nudge forward.

"I hope you didn't talk too many of the kids into joining the Army," she quipped. She pumped her legs, like she had when she was five, and got the swing to go higher.

Jake took a step backward. When her back met his hands again, he smoothly pushed her forward. "Naw, new rules say they have to finish high school first."

As Jake continued to push her, Ali began to feel like she could swing in the schoolyard forever with Jake. All she needed was a flowing white dress, some flowers in her hair, and a day that would never end.

But that was another Norman Rockwell painting that would never get done.

She dragged her feet in the soft sand that covered the play area and brought the swing to an abrupt stop. Jake circled and faced her.

"Are you hungry?" she asked him.

"I could eat."

Ali gestured to the penguin suit. "I have to get this back to the county first, but then I could take off a couple of comp hours and we could catch a late lunch or early dinner," she suggested.

"I'd like that," Jake replied. "Tell me where to meet you." He picked the suit up from the merry-go-round on which it was perched and walked with her toward the parking lot.

"It will take me about an hour to get everything squared away," she said. "Are you familiar with the area?"

"A little."

"We can meet at the mall. There's a nice seafood restaurant there. It shouldn't be crowded this time of the day, so we won't need reservations."

"I know that one," Jake said. "It's a plan." He opened

the passenger-side door of Ali's car and set the suit on the seat. "So I'll see you in about an hour?" he asked.

Ali opened the driver's-side door. "I'll see you in one hour and not a minute later."

Chapter Eight

As soon as Ali turned into the parking deck at the mall, her heartbeat skyrocketed. All she could seem to think about was that, in about five minutes, she'd be with Jake again. She saw an empty parking slot next to the elevator and headed right for it, barely beating an SUV heading for the same space.

She waved as the owner of the car blew the horn when she eased her car into PARK. She grimaced when she saw his face in her rearview mirror. He looked mighty angry. Oh well, she'd gotten there first, maybe by disobeying the posted 5 MPH sign to make sure of it.

But a girl had to do what a girl had to do. Jake was waiting.

As she walked down the stairs to the restaurant level, she could almost feel the blood race around in her veins. What on earth had taken hold of her anyway? She couldn't remember feeling this giddy since she'd been ten and on a family vacation to Universal Studios in

Florida. She'd turned a corner at the theme park and walked right into her hero, Wolverine, from the X-Men comics. Or rather, she'd walked into an actor playing Wolverine for the day.

But she hadn't cared. It was during her tomboy stage, and she and her best friend in the whole world, Tommy, were into collecting comic books and watching sci-fi. Tommy had moved away the next year and left her alone to outgrow superheroes. She smiled at the memory and picked up her pace. The real-life hero she was about to meet for dinner was a lot more interesting than an actor in black spandex—unless, of course, that actor was Hugh Jackman.

In the next second, the memory of Jake Daultry down on one knee talking to a first-grader flashed through her mind. No, she decided. Jake in his olive drab dress uniform was a lot sexier than Hugh Jackman, even Hugh Jackman in black spandex.

She shook her head. She'd only known Jake for three days, and already he filled every space in her mind.

Why in the world did she follow the impulse to lean over and kiss him when they left the party? Because when it came to being spontaneous, she was just like her mother, she answered herself.

Kissing Jake had definitely made things a bit more complicated. But it wasn't entirely her fault. She wasn't the only one doing the kissing that day. He had kissed her first, and had called upon God and country to do it—not that he'd needed to.

As she maneuvered down the last staircase, she wrestled with placing the blame on him for the way she was feeling. By the time she reached the bottom-level landing and turned the corner onto the restaurant level, she decided that even her hair hurt from the battle.

But being slightly angry quickly turned to an emotion she barely recognized when she saw Jake talking to four girls she guessed were early college age. They were taking turns posing with him and taking pictures with their cell phones. Remembering how easily the charm seemed to flow, she couldn't help but wonder what Jake was up to now.

The redhead had just leaned into him, waiting for her friend to take the shot, when he noticed Ali. He waited until the picture was taken before he acknowledged her.

"What are you doing?" she asked him, carefully controlling the volume of her voice as he walked to her. She knew she screeched when she was angry, and for some reason, she was as angry as heck seeing him with four women.

"Bye, Jake," one of them cooed. She waved to him as all four began to walk away.

He waved back.

"Thanks for the pictures," another said.

"They'll be up on my Facebook page if you want to see them," the brunet with blond streaks in her hair called. "My name is Anna Brown. Send me a friend request." She gestured at Ali. "You can too."

"Oh, I'll rush right home," Ali said, her voice lathered in sarcasm.

"They were just being friendly while I waited for you," Jake explained.

Ali leaned back and crossed her arms. "Oh, they were being friendly, huh? They were simply doing their patriotic duty, I suppose?"

"It's the uniform that gets all the attention."

"Uh-huh, I can see how that would happen."

"Honest," Jake protested. "I was waiting for you when one of them walked up to me and asked if she could take a picture with me."

"And why was that?"

Jake shrugged. "I guess I'll have to check her Facebook page to find out."

Ali narrowed her eyes at him.

"Why, Ms. Archer, I do believe you're jealous."

She opened her mouth to debate the point and then stopped. Was that what she'd felt when she'd seen him with the girls? She pulled her eyebrows down in a frown. Wow, she was in bad shape.

"I am not jealous. I am hungry," she said instead. "I am told outward signs are similar." She pointed to the seafood restaurant closest to them. "Shall we go inside before a Brownie troop comes by and makes you their badge project?"

"Yes, let's do that." He crooked his arm, and she took it.

Inside, the hostess grabbed two menus and began to lead them to a table.

"What about one of these?" Jake asked stopping by a series of small tables along one of the walls. The tables were set inside partitioned niches with floor-to-ceiling drapes tied back on either side.

"You'd like one of our cozies?" the hostess asked.

Jake looked at Ali and tossed his head toward them. "It'll be quieter inside."

Ali looked at the intimate setting. It would give them a little privacy in the busy restaurant. "Why not?" she agreed. "At least it will be harder for your entourage to find you."

They sat down and the hostess handed them their menus, explaining that a server would be over soon.

Jake looked around the snug little niche. "This is nice." His gaze traveled over her face and settled on her eyes. "It's almost like no one else is here but us."

Ali picked up the menu and pretended to read. If he kept looking at her like that she was going to explode. Outside in the mall, she'd felt as though she had been sharing Jake with all the shoppers. Here in the cozy, it did seem as though it was just them, one on one.

She thought back to the college girls. She really couldn't blame them. What women wouldn't want some tangible memento of her time with Jake? In his uniform, he looked the emblematic all-American hero, the kind you'd see in a recruiting film on TV. With his broad shoulders and even broader smile, she had no doubt that he could fill any woman's fantasy of the dashing soldier swooping in to save the world.

The incredible love scene from the movie *Ryan's Daughter* raced through her mind, transporting her from a restaurant in New Jersey to Ireland during World War I. Just like now, in the movie, amid a time full of activity, the lovers were alone. Those lovers had been in a forest, with sunlight streaming through the branches, spider webs glistening, and dandelions swaying. It would be easy for her mind's eye to cast herself as the Irish girl and Jake as the British soldier. For her it was the most passionate, heartfelt love scene ever burned onto film.

For her own good, she dragged her gaze away from his sparkling eyes. "The crab cakes are wonderful here."

He folded his menu and set it on the table. "That's good enough for me."

As promised, the server promptly came by and took their orders. Just as promptly, he returned with two glasses of iced tea with lemon wedges draped over the brim. Ali picked hers up from the table and took a healthy drink. Ogling Jake had made her mighty thirsty.

"So . . ." Jake said pulling in a small breath. "Were you jealous outside?"

"Hardly," Ali protested. She felt her cheeks warm with the little white lie.

"I think you were."

"Don't be so smug," Ali warned. "I told you I was hungry. They were cutting into my meal time."

He reached for a dinner roll the server brought to the table along with the drinks. "Mm-hmm, I think I was right."

"Maybe you were."

Jake let the softly spoken word hang in the air. He could tell from her body language and the hint of pink on her cheeks that the *maybe* was actually a *yes*. He wanted to lean across the table and kiss her senseless for the admission. It validated that she was attracted to him and that was a big thing. It was good to know that he was not alone in what he was feeling. It gave what was happening between them a more equal balance.

It made him want to pursue something he had strictly avoided most of his life. It made him want to see if something deeper could happen between them in the short amount of time he had to give her.

"Your family sure is interesting."

"That is an understatement."

"I liked the way you all go at each other. It tells me that you're close."

Ali tipped back her head. "I guess that's one way to look at it."

"So now, it seems, everyone is settled except you."

"Yep," Ali agreed, "so far."

He leaned forward and lowered his voice. "How do you feel about soldiers?"

The question took her by surprise. "I really don't know all that much except for what I see on the news."

"I don't mean those soldiers." He extended his hand, palm down, in an invitation for her to take it. "I mean this soldier."

She looked first at his hand and then at him.

Jake withdrew his hand. "I mean, I came into your life like a tank, I just wonder what you are thinking."

Ali reigned in her reckless impulse to tell him. "I don't believe in whirlwind romances, if that's what you mean."

"You don't really know me. I understand."

"And you don't know me. I could be a serial killer or something."

Jake laughed. "I don't know many serial killers who want to save the world one aluminum can at a time."

He saw Ali's cheeks flush a soft pink. That was twice in about ten minutes he had gotten her to blush. In these aggressive, open times there weren't many women who blushed anymore. He loved it that he had that kind of physical effect on her.

"You know a lot more about me than I do about you."

"Soldiers have to be able to gather intelligence on a subject quickly."

"I suppose."

"In combat, you have to reconnoiter the situation and react in an instant. There isn't much leeway for a wrong decision."

Ali leaned back as the server placed their food on the table. "Have you seen much combat?"

"Let's just say that I've seen more than I'd like," Jake acknowledged.

"Then why don't you get out?"

Jake didn't hesitate. "I love what I do."

Ali cut a piece of crab cake with her fork. "And what is it, exactly, that you do? I know you fly helicopters, but beyond that, I'm not sure."

"I pilot an H-60 Black Hawk. It's the Army's front-line utility helicopter used for air assault, air cavalry, and aeromedical evacs."

"Which one do you do?"

"Lately, I've been doing a lot of evacs."

"And what were you doing before that?"

"I flew soldiers into combat. I dropped them off and picked them up after the mission was over."

"Have you ever shot at anyone?"

"Not while I was flying, I haven't, but I have been shot at while in the air."

Ali felt a wave of anxiety wash over her. "That sounds scary."

"Don't worry. The Black Hawk can tolerate small-arms fire and most medium-caliber explosive projectiles. The critical systems are armored or made to withstand multiple small-arms hits."

"Like the parts around where the pilots sit—those parts are armored?"

"Some of it is."

"How did you feel when you were fired upon?" Her voice fell to a whisper. "Were you scared?"

Jake shrugged. "It's part of the job."

Ali sat back. "As I said, why then, don't you just get out?" She saw the look on Jake's face turn from conversational cheerful to serious in what she suspected was a mere nanosecond.

"Before *you* can save the world, Ali, *I* have to be sure there is still a world to save."

She looked at him, open-mouthed, silent.

"Say something," he prompted after a few minutes.

"I can't."

"Why can't you?"

"I can't argue with the truth, although every cell in my body is annoyed about it."

"You've never been at a loss for words?"

She shook her head. "This is the first time."

He leaned forward and slid his elbows onto the table. "Then I intend to savor the moment for as long as I can." Jake could see that there was a moment while thoughts crossed Ali's expressive eyes. Then a sparkle began in their green depth and a smile teased the corner of her lips, catching his attention even more.

She mimicked his movement, leaning toward him. "Enjoy it soldier-boy, because I intend not to let it happen again."

"We'll see about that." He paused for emphasis, and then added, "Treehugger."

Ali's eyes sparkled with enthusiasm and her lips parted wide in a smile that showed her teeth. Jake had a wild, swift desire to keep that look on her face as long as possible. He enjoyed their sparring immensely, and could think of only one way at the moment to keep it going.

He leaned across the table and kissed her.

"Ali Archer, is that you?"

Even as close as they were, Jake could see Ali's eye widen. She jerked backward and looked to her left.

"Mrs. Meyers, Mrs. Brown, I didn't see you there."

"I would imagine not, dear. You and the young man were kissing," Mrs. Meyers remarked.

"In *public*," Mrs. Brown added, emphasizing her displeasure with an added tick.

"Captain Daultry had something in his eye," Ali said weakly.

"Yes, your eyelash," Mrs. Brown quickly cut in. "And it was still attached to your eyelid, I might add."

Ali did her best to ignore the comment. She pasted on a smile. "Jake, these are two of my mother's friends, Angela Meyers and Carol Brown."

Jake quickly stood. "Ladies, please don't get the

wrong impression of Ms. Archer. It was all my fault." He took a step out of the niche. "I was just telling her about how much I missed the good old USA, and how much I appreciated her helping me before I had to go back."

"Go back?" Mrs. Meyers asked.

"Yes, I'll be returning to the Middle East."

"Oh my," Mrs. Meyers said. She turned to her friend. "Isn't Margie's grandson serving in the Army there?"

"I do believe so," Mrs. Brown returned.

"Ladies," Jake cut in, "if you can get me his name, I'd be happy to look him up once I get back."

"That would be lovely," Mrs. Meyers said, pulling a notepad from her purse and writing down a name. She handed it to Jake. "He enlisted right out of high school, and Margie is really concerned for him."

Jake took it from her. "Ma'am, we take care of our own there," he assured. "I'll find out where he is and how he's doing. Can you write down a number where I can get in touch with his grandmother once I do?"

"Oh my, yes," Mrs. Meyers said, quickly adding the phone number to the name. She handed it back to Jake and turned to Ali. "I am so glad I ran into you and your boyfriend today. Margie will feel a lot better knowing someone is looking after her grandson."

Knowing that Angela Meyers was to gossip what Thomas Edison was to the telephone, Ali quickly countered, "He's a friend, not my boyfriend."

"Of course, I can see that, dear. And do tell your mother we were asking about her," Mrs. Meyers said. Then she started to walk to her table.

"Did you see all his medals?" she heard Mrs. Brown ask.

"He did have quite a few," Mrs. Meyers agreed.

Mrs. Brown turned back to look at Jake and Ali once more. "Yes, he did, and I'll bet not one of them was for good conduct."

Ali dropped her head into her hands as Jake sat back down.

"What's wrong?" he asked. "I think that went rather well."

Ali watched the hostess seat Mrs. Meyers and Mrs. Brown at a table with a direct sight line to the cozy.

"Do you see where they are sitting?"

Jake looked over at the women. They waved at him at the same time.

"Do you think it is a coincidence that they're sitting where they can see us?"

"Doesn't the hostess pick the table?"

Ali raised her eyes to the ceiling and shook her head. "You *have* been out of the country too long. They asked to sit there, as sure as I was named after a New Jersey state park."

Jake whipped his head around. "You were what?"

Ali wiped away the question with a swipe of her hand. "Never mind." Suddenly a mischievous grin crossed her face.

Jake couldn't help but notice it. "What are you up to, Ali?"

"I'm going to give those two something to really tell Mom. Don't ask any questions—just do what I do." She reached out and unhooked the drape on her side of the cozy. It fluttered down and blocked half the view. "Now it's your turn."

Jake could see the women were staring intently. He couldn't resist. He waggled his fingers at them just before he shut the rest of the curtain.

"There," Ali said smugly. "They were going to call Mom anyway. Now they really have something to tell her."

Chapter Nine

Ali pulled into the driveway of her town house and waited until the automatic opener finished raising the garage door. She pulled inside, the headlights from Jake's car illuminating the garage when he pulled into the driveway behind her. As the door continued its way down, she got out of the car and walked into the house through the connecting kitchen door.

After sprinting through the kitchen and down the hall, she tossed her purse into the office off the living room and checked the condition of her hair in the hallway mirror. Okay, it was nice, but not perfect. The penguin head had given her a sort of "hat head," but it was too late to worry about that now. She'd just spent two hours in a curtain-draped cozy with Jake. He couldn't have missed it if he'd tried.

She walked to the front door and pulled it open. Jake was leaning against the wrought iron railing, arms crossed over his chest. "I missed you," he said.

She shook her head and opened the door wider. "You don't have to flirt with me. You got my attention."

"I wasn't flirting. I was being honest. I missed you."

Ali laughed as Jake wrapped his arms around her waist once he was inside the door. He spun her around until her back was against solid oak.

"You can't miss someone you just met a few days ago."

Raising his hands, he placed them palms flat against the door on either side of her head. Then he leaned in, effectively pinning her in place. "Yes, you can," he corrected.

Smiling up at him, she smoothed her palms up his chest until her fingers found the medal ribbons on his jacket. She outlined the three rows with her fingertip. "You must have done some amazing things to get these," she whispered.

Jake tilted his chin down and looked at her hands. "Some people might say that." Her chin still down, he looked back up at her from between thick, dark lashes. "What do you think?"

She slid her hands down his ribcage until she reached his stomach, the taut muscles of his abdomen flexing with her touch. Then she pushed forward with all her might. "I think Mrs. Brown was right. None of those medals were for good conduct."

He blinked a few times as though he was confused, but then got the message and freed her. "Sorry, was I acting too aggressive?"

"For only knowing someone for a few days, yes, you were. I've seen *M*A*S*H*. I am not R and R in Tokyo."

"And I'm not Hawkeye Pierce," he defended. His face turned serious. "It may only be a few days since we met, but I feel something. I think you do too." As if he could read her thoughts, his gaze traveled over her face.

"Maybe I feel something," she admitted.

One dark eyebrow quirked. "So what do you call this feeling—attraction?"

"It could be—but it could also be heartburn after running into Mom's friends at dinner."

His laughter came easily. "I can understand that."

For a few heartbeats, Ali stayed where she was. "Want to come in for a few minutes?" She took a step backward to allow some more room between them.

"I was hoping you'd ask." He followed her inside, unbuttoning his jacket. "Mind if I take this off? I feel very military and formal with it on."

She turned to him. "Please make yourself comfortable."

She took the jacket from his hand. The open floor plan of her town house allowed access to the dining room from the front door, and she could feel him watching her as she draped the jacket over the back of one of the dining room chairs. When she turned back to him, she saw he'd taken a seat on the far end of the couch.

"So, if not 'Hawkeye,' what do they call you in your unit?" she asked, walking to join him in the living room.

Jake's lips quirked. "I hope they call me Captain, mostly."

"Very funny. But that's not what I meant, and you know it. I thought all pilots had some sort of macho nickname. I was just curious as to what yours might be."

" 'Mountie'—that's what they call me," he replied.

Ali stopped short of sitting and shifted away in surprise. "Your nickname isn't something tough-sounding, like Ace or Slayer or Assassin?"

"Nope, I'm Mountie because I always get my man."

She grabbed a pillow and settled into the corner of the couch. "I have got to hear this."

"I said I always get my man, but it's not in the way you think."

"Mountie does sound more like someone in the Military Police, and you're a helicopter pilot. So how did you get that tag?"

He took a deep breath and began. "I work out of Balad Air Base about sixty miles north of Baghdad. My job is simple. I have to evacuate anyone injured on the battlefield as quickly as possible. But getting to the jobsite is the real problem." He looked at her. "Are you sure you want to hear this?"

Ali bit down on her bottom lip and nodded.

"Around midnight is usually when it gets busy inside the operations center. It seems like every half hour an alert comes in. All the radio traffic is monitored on a Speak & Spell. It's a kind of instant messaging system attached to an electronic voice. As soon as an injury report comes in, the clock starts ticking. The dispatcher on duty grabs a walkie-talkie and alerts the crew on call to get moving."

Ali straightened and leaned closer to him, interested but remaining silent.

"If a soldier survives an attack, after the medic patches

him up, if he can get to a facility within the first hour, his chance of survival is over ninety-five percent."

"And that's where you come in," Ali offered.

Jake nodded. "I make sure that within three minutes of the call I'm in the Black Hawk and ready to power it up. I want to be airborne within five minutes, and on my way to the injured."

"Can you do that so quickly?"

"I try. I can never sleep when I'm on call, no matter if I've been on duty all day or all night. Once I hear the dispatcher's voice shouting 'Medevac' on the two-way, the adrenaline starts pumping and I head for the chopper. While I'm waiting for the rest of my crew, the on-duty at the operations center and I go over an electronic map of Iraq that shows the red sectors he's been studying."

"What are red sectors?"

"They're the danger zones, areas where helicopters are most likely to come under fire."

Ali's eyes widened and her hands gripped the pillow tighter.

"We have pretty good recon, and information is updated frequently," he said reassuringly, "so we can pretty much find the fastest route possible to get to the soldiers."

"Does he also help find the safest way to get there?"

"It doesn't matter if it's safe or not. It has to be the fastest. Someone is hurt and the clock is ticking. As soon as the crew is in the Hawk, we're up and moving east over the grid coordinates."

"What's it like?" Ali asked in a small voice.

"Inside the cabin is dark, but outside the pitch blackness is usually illuminated by red streaks of tracer fire and the occasional flash from a gun muzzle."

Ali's mouth dropped open, and reaching out, Jake touched her hand. "Should I stop?"

She shook her head again.

"When we get to the field, the night seems to get even blacker. Even with night vision goggles, it's hard to find a place to land. We know someone is out there waiting for us, and every minute we can't touch down seems like an hour."

"Do you ever get shot at while you're looking?"

"We do. The painted red cross on the side of the chopper means nothing to anyone who wants to shoot it down."

"Aren't you vulnerable then?"

"We are, but the medic and the crew chief double as chopper security, leaning out the windows and scanning the ground for insurgents. Mostly, though, they hope no one is aiming at us. One we find a place to put down, the medic jumps out to hook up with the ground contact."

"Isn't there anyone else inside to help cover you?"

"We'd rather have the room for the injured. Sometimes you expect one and get three. You can't be sure there hasn't been a sniper or something while you've been en-route."

Ali drew her brows together in thought and almost stopped there. "What happens next?" she hesitantly asked.

"Soldiers bring the litter to the chopper. It's too loud to actually talk to them, so we can't ask the extent of the injuries, but we know that it's been about fifteen minutes since the person lying on the litter has been shot or come into contact with an explosive of some type. We just secure the litter and go top speed. My objective at that point is for the patient not to die in my aircraft."

"And has anyone?" Ali asked in a small voice.

"A few times," Jake admitted. "But we do whatever we can to make sure that we keep the patient alive until he can get a higher level of care and better treatment than we can provide in the chopper with the little equipment we have. I try to make sure that, within as little time as possible, the soldier is inside the trauma ward at the base. The hospital there is one of the most advanced combat field hospitals in history. Once I get him there, it's up to a Higher Power to decide what happens next."

Ali's eyes flicked upward in response. "I can't imagine doing that day after day. It must be hard on the emotions."

"You have to leave your emotions behind when you take off. It's all automatic from that point on. It has to be. The guys are counting on you doing your job by the book."

"What if the book is wrong?"

He shook his head. "You can't second-guess a decision. There's no time for that. With every tick, a life is in the balance, and that balance can go either way."

Ali pressed her lips together. Listening to the news about the Middle East was one thing, but looking into

Jake's eyes as he spoke about his job was another. The raw emotion, the commitment, and the feeling of honor in serving one's country mixed together and exploded in a display of passion more vivid that a Fourth of July celebration.

But there was something else in his eyes, something he hadn't talked about.

She took his hand. "The book isn't always right, is it?"

At her touch, Jake almost recoiled, but Ali felt the reaction and held on tighter. He looked from her hand to her face. "It's not something I like to dwell on."

"You shouldn't keep it inside, Jake."

He looked back to her hand, so small around his but seeming like a lifeline. "It's an unavoidable part of war, Ali." She squeezed his hand as though she wanted to let him know that she understood.

"It's unavoidable, but terrible."

With her free hand, she cupped his cheek. At the contact, he looked up into her eyes. She could see the pain eat away at every other emotion she had seen there, and the sight hit her hard. Sensing tears building, she blinked to hold them back.

She broke contact with him and got his uniform jacket. After sitting back down, she draped it across her lap and ran her fingertips across the service ribbons. "Tell me about some of them."

"Do you really want to know?"

She nodded. "Yes, I do. This one—it looks like a rainbow—why did you get it?"

"It's the Army Service Ribbon. We get it for completing training."

Ali nodded. "And what is this one?"

"It's an Iraq Campaign Medal Ribbon."

She was about to point to another when her eye was drawn to the one ribbon she hadn't considered. She ran her fingers over it: the Purple Heart Medal Ribbon.

"You were wounded." The words came out in a rush of air.

Jake nodded but said nothing.

Ali grew very still as she saw Jake struggle to speak on such a highly emotional topic. "What happened?" she urged him softly.

Jake stared off into the distance. "It was night. The crew chief spotted a few insurgents with the night goggles just as we were loading the stretcher into the back. It wasn't like anything we'd encountered before. I guess they had just gotten some updated equip because it seemed that every shot that came at us hit its target." His throat constricted, the words strained. "I hollered back for them to get low. The shots were coming from all sides. I heard a ping to my left and then felt the burn in my shoulder. I hung in there until the medic told me the wounded were secure, and then I just bugged out of there."

The terrible feeling that Jake could have been killed overwhelmed Ali. Her fingers tightened around his jacket. The suffering in Jake's eyes brought tears again to hers, but she fought them back.

"You got the men back to the base in time?"

"For most of them," Jake said hoarsely. "One of them didn't make it." He shut his eyes and Ali could see a faint line of moisture in their corners. "If only I could have flown faster, but the pain in my shoulder made my head swim at times. I had to take it easy or risk losing everyone if I crashed."

Reaching over, Ali placed her hand on his arm and felt his muscles tense beneath her fingertips. "Jake, you did everything you could." Her fingers tightened when he looked at her, and she could see tears bead on his lashes. The realization that he trusted her enough to show his emotions shook her deeply.

Forcing back his tears, Jake blinked hard, wildly aware of Ali's hand on his arm. Her touch was electric and dredged up more than he had ever felt for someone before. He wanted to find his way into her arms, but contained himself. She was right. They had only known each other for a few days. But to him it could have been a lifetime. His connection to her had fused like a weld.

He saw tears trail down her cheeks in silver paths that told him that she understood his pain. The realization was like first aid to his bruised heart.

"You're amazing," he said. He took her hand and held it tightly. With it, she fed him strength, a sense that it was safe for him to show how much it affected him. With Ali he was home, and he knew it.

Sniffing, Ali reached up and brushed the tears from her eyes. "I'm sorry. I didn't mean for you to have to relive that."

Jake captured her other hand, stopping her from wiping away any more tears. Then he let it go and wiped them for her with his fingertips. "I'm sorry I made you cry."

Ali looked down at their hands. Jake's long fingers were darkly tanned from the time spent in the Iraqi sun. Hers were small and glaringly white against his skin. That was only another reminder of their differences.

Jake bowed his head. "For a second there, I thought I was going to lose it."

"Maybe you should have."

Jake shook his head. "I have to stay in control. I can't let it out and jeopardize the mission."

"But you're not on duty. You're home."

The pain in Jake's chest widened. How could she understand? Stroking her hand, he felt the firm softness of her skin beneath his. "Now, I'd like to hear a little about you," he said, changing the subject.

Ali smiled. "Are you sure you would?"

"I want to hear all about your family and why you were named after a state park. I want to know all about the woman who dresses like a huge penguin and buys her three-month-old nephew a drum set."

A tremor of panic ran through Ali. How easy it would be to fall into Jake's eyes and drown in the caring he was showing her now. How easy it would be to fall into his arms and kiss him and stoke the fire of awareness that she could see in his eyes.

Maybe she should, she thought. Maybe she could be his, albeit for only thirty days. How wrong could it be?

Then, just as quickly as the thought came, it left her.

What on earth was she doing? He had a job to do thousands of miles away, and she couldn't let him think about her while he was doing it. One distraction, one errant thought could cost him his life. She wouldn't, couldn't take that chance—with either of their hearts. "You've given me a lot to think about," she said.

"I didn't come over here to do that. I just wanted to get to know you better."

"That's quite a compliment coming from a real-life hero."

"I'm not a hero, Ali. I'm just a guy doing what has to be done. If I didn't, some other pilot would."

"Be careful. Modesty is a very sexy trait, you know."

Jake smiled. "You really think so?"

"Oh, yes—I really think so."

"We're good for each other, Ali."

"Sometimes," she agreed. "But when it comes right down to it, I'm a rabid environmentalist and a free-speaking, free-thinking person, and you're"—she looked at him sadly—"not. You're button-down military. You're my complete opposite." Ali blew out a long breath. "I'm sorry. It's none of my business how you have to do your job."

"Sure it is," Jake assured her. "We like each other, so we're naturally concerned about one another." He patted her hand. "Listen, it's late. I'd better go." He rose from the couch. "Try not to miss me," he quipped.

"It'll be hard not to," Ali said drolly. She stood and handed him his jacket. "You're growing on me."

She saw the intensity in his eyes change and knew that he was going to kiss her. His eyes narrowed and her breath caught in her throat. The jacket fell from his hands, and she felt his arms go around her.

Contact with him was galvanizing. She closed her eyes and he drew her against him. His moist breath caressed her cheek as he leaned toward her. Her lips parted, and she surrendered to his arms when she heard her name coming from him the second before his lips claimed hers.

His kiss was as powerful as he was. His lips, firm and warm, moved against hers as he slid his hands down her back to her waist. His lips moved to her cheek and then to her throat. She tilted her head and inhaled the warm scent of him, a heady combination of citrus and man.

When his mouth returned to her lips, he kissed her so deeply that her knees buckled a little, and she held on to his arms for support. He kissed her and whispered her name again, his lips brushing against an ear.

Leaning against him in perfect relaxation, her senses felt tuned to his voice, his scent, and his touch. She floated blissfully in a seemingly hypnotized surrender, enjoying feelings she had never experienced with anyone before. When he stepped back and took her hands again, she gazed at him, her heart still pounding erratically in her chest.

"I won't forget that," she assured him.

Jake chuckled softly. "That was my plan." His gaze roamed her face. "I like what I see in your eyes."

"And just what do you see?" she asked, her voice a whisper.

"I see that you like me." Stopping himself from touching her again, he stepped back. "I'll call you tomorrow."

"You don't have a phone."

"The electronics store opens at eight A.M."

"Then you had better be first in line."

They walked to her front door arm in arm. There he placed a chaste kiss on her forehead. "Good night, Ali."

"Good night, Jake." She wanted to say more, but the words lodged in her throat. She didn't want him to leave. She wanted him to stay. But stay and do what—talk, watch movies, kiss until dawn?

Confused by so many rich emotions brought on by his kiss, she wasn't quite sure. So she decided to say nothing for right now. She'd figure it out in the morning, when she had time to think.

Jake left after one gentler kiss. She went to the sofa and dropped down into it. Grabbing the pillow, she pressed it against her stomach and sank into the corner. How long she sat there, lost in remembering his kiss, she didn't know, but when she looked at the clock it was 1:00 A.M., and she knew she had to try to get some sleep. Work loomed in the morning, with a staff meeting first thing.

Once in bed, she stared at the play of shadows on her ceiling thinking about Jake. Everything he told her swirled inside her mind. He had been wounded in action but didn't think of anything but his mission and getting the men back to the base and to the field hospital. Until today, she had never thought of the war in the Middle East in any terms except what was reported on the evening news.

Now, however, it was personal. Jake could have been killed. Everything in her life seemed to pale in comparison to that.

She knew she had feelings for him, and that those

feelings had intensified today. It would be hard for any-one not to be overwhelmed by what he had told her. It would be hard for anyone not to feel admiration and pride for a man like him.

Another question suddenly bubbled up inside her: Was she falling for Jake, or for the patriotic heart tugging and appeal of his being a soldier?

And could she trust him with her heart when he left her for another eleven-month tour of duty? Would the in-tense attraction they felt now survive a separation of thousands of miles?

If their relationship was going to go any further, she would have to make sure she knew the answers to her questions—for both of their sakes.

Chapter Ten

Normally, on the third Thursday of the month, when Tess Archer insisted that the entire family get together for dinner, it didn't bother Ali at all. But nothing was ordinary when you were an Archer, and this wasn't an ordinary third Thursday.

It was the one after she'd met Jake Daultry.

And it was the one after the two biggest gossips in the world had seen her with Jake at the mall.

There was no way in the world they didn't run back and call her mother to tell Tess all about it. But Ali hadn't heard from her mother all day. That was not a good sign. To Ali, it meant that Tess was going to interrogate her in front of Trent and Somer.

Who didn't love a family inquisition?

When Ali pulled onto her mom's street, Trent and Somer's cars were already in the driveway. *Great,* she thought, *they've all had a head start planning what to say to me.* With Trent being a police officer and Somer still working for the newspaper off and on, she could imagine what was in store for her. They didn't need the hot lights of an interrogation room. Three pairs of eyes would make it warm enough.

She got out of her car and walked to the front door. With a silent vow to not to make it easy for them, she stepped inside.

The aroma of meatloaf filled the air. She should have known. In the Archer household, meatloaf was like a truth serum. She didn't know what her mother put in it, but with enough of it inside you, you couldn't help but talk.

She could hear pots clanging in the kitchen. She hung her coat on one of the hooks by the door and stashed her purse on a chair in the living room. She walked into the kitchen to see Trent washing salad greens in the sink. No one else was around.

She saw some chicken frying on the stove. "I see Mom's still indulging you," Ali said to him. "You never did like Mom's meatloaf once you caught on to its hidden powers."

"Ever since we had it every day for a week until I told her that I copied Samantha Jones' paper in math class, I swore another piece of meatloaf would never pass my lips. That stuff could make every terrorist in the world confess and convert," he acknowledged.

"Funny, but Somer and I don't have a problem with it."

"That's because estrogen blocks whatever she puts in it."

Ali laughed. "It wasn't the meatloaf, Trent. It was the

note the vice principal sent home telling Mom what you did."

Trent let the strainer fall into the sink and turned around to face her. "Why didn't you ever tell me that?"

"Because it was so much fun to watch all your machinations trying to get out of eating meatloaf until Mom got tired of them too and started making chicken for you. After that, I just kind of forgot."

"Good, then I'll have some today."

"Of course, I could be wrong." She leveled a serious look at him. "Done anything you wouldn't want Mom to know about?"

"Maybe I won't have any," he quickly added.

Ali looked around. "Where is everyone?"

"Upstairs somewhere," Trent answered. "Mom wanted to pull out our baby pictures and see who Michael looked more like."

Ali watched him rinse more lettuce for the salad and knew better than to offer to help. Trent was a master at getting someone else to do things he didn't like to do, and cooking was one of them.

"Linda here?" she asked her brother.

He shook his head. "No, she's taking another class at NYU."

Ali ruffled her brother's hair. "Better watch out or someday she's finally going to realize that she's eons ahead of you and run off with some PhD or something."

Trent aimed the spray nozzle at her, trying to give her a quick spritz. Ali ducked in time and the water sprayed harmlessly on the kitchen table.

"I don't suppose you'd be willing to clean that up?"

he asked, nodding toward the water-soaked tablecloth as she lifted the lid off the pot containing the sauce bubbling on the stove.

"I don't think so. You made the mess."

"But you ducked. If you hadn't, the water would be on you."

"Quite so, but then you'd have another problem on your hands, brother dear."

An impish grin crossed Trent's face. "If I were you, I'd be more worried about the problem you're going to have explaining what you did at the mall yesterday." He put the strainer down in the sink and closed the curtains on the kitchen window. "Oh, does this look familiar, sis?"

Ali's eyes narrowed. She knew she should have gotten to her mother's house sooner. She had provided her mother, sister, and brother with far too much alone time to concoct some piece of fiction as to what happened during dinner. But she was not going to fall into Trent's trap of trying to get her to talk about it now.

"Not really," she said in the calmest voice she could produce. She slid out a kitchen chair and threw herself down into it. "Why do you ask?"

"I hear those cozies at the restaurant are nice and private."

Ali rested her elbow on the table and propped her chin on her hand. "And just what would prompt that comment?" Maybe she could find out just how much Mrs. Brown or Mrs. Meyers had told her mother.

"Word is you wanted to be alone with a certain soldier in one last night."

"Whose word is it?"

Trent turned and rested his hip on edge of the counter as he dried his hands with a dishtowel. "Ali, Ali, Ali," he said, shaking his head. "Don't you know by now that there are no secrets here? If I were you, I'd volunteer the info before Mom has a chance to grill you. It would be less painful that way."

Ali's eyes flared. "It's your fault."

Trent put a hand on his chest. "Surely you don't mean *moi*?"

"Yes, I mean you. If you weren't getting married in three months, I could have a nice quiet date with a guy and it wouldn't cause the phone lines to heat up."

"You know my getting married has nothing to do with that. Those two are just biddies."

"Yes, but if you weren't getting married, phase two of the deadly rings wouldn't be in play, and I wouldn't be last on the list."

"What list would that be, dear?"

Tess Archer walked into the living room carrying her grandson. Somer followed close behind her.

"The isn't-he-the-cutest-baby-in-the-world list," Ali said, standing up and holding out her arms. "Give that little sweetheart to me."

Tess transferred Michael to Ali and draped a receiving blanket over her shoulder. Ali kissed both of Michael's cheeks and then rested him against her chest. His head bobbed on her shoulder.

"He's a strong one, isn't he?" Tess asked with pride. "See how he holds up his head?" She nodded to her son. "You were a strong baby, Trent. I guess it's an Archer trait."

Good, Ali thought. Get her talking about Michael. "Did you find the pictures, Mom?"

"They're right here." Somer held up the photo album as Tess walked over to the stove and checked on dinner.

"Did you decide who he looks more like?" Ali asked, trying to make sure the conversation stayed on her nephew.

"We think he looks like his father," Somer said, "more like a Daultry than an Archer."

"Which reminds me," Tess said, reaching into the kitchen cabinet to get out her every day dishes, "how was your dinner with Jake?" She smiled at her daughter as she set out four plates at the table.

Ali moved Michael back into her arms so she could see his face. "You think he looks like Nick? I think he looks more like us."

"Jake bears a strong resemblance to Nick, don't you think, Ali?" Tess pressed.

"I do," Trent volunteered. "I never could understand how you didn't know he was family when you first met him." He dug into the silverware drawer and helped set the table. "That would have been something to watch, don't you think, Somer?"

Somer looked at Ali and saw the pleading in her sister's eyes. "Why don't we have dinner and let Ali tell us in her own time?" She held out her hands.

Ali mouthed "thanks" as she handed over her nephew to his mother.

"I'll settle Michael into the portacrib and set up the baby monitor and be right back." She began to walk into the living room, but turned. "I wouldn't miss her explanation for anything." With a laugh evil enough to be included in a horror film, she left to complete her task.

Ali dropped her head and extended her hands, wrists together in a gesture she knew her brother would recognize. "I give up. You win"—she snapped her head up—"for the moment."

"How did this water get here?" Tess asked pointing to the table.

"He did it."

"She did it."

Trent and Ali said the words in unison.

Tess took a dishtowel from the kitchen drawer next to the sink. "You two," she said as she wiped the table dry. Then she walked to the sink and handed the dishtowel to Trent. "Of all of you, you and Ali were the closest. I hope that doesn't change too much when you get married," she said to him. Tess motioned for Somer to sit when she came back into the room.

Trent hung the dishtowel on the oven door handle. "Yes, Ali will soon be the only one without a significant other." He grinned broadly at his baby sister.

Ali waited until her mother turned to stir the spaghetti sauce before mouthing the words "you are so dead."

"Unless Jake is in the picture," Somer reminded everybody.

"*Et tu, Brute?*" Ali whispered.

"I do what I can," Somer said with a smile.

Done with the dinner preparation, Tess began to dish out healthy portions. "I have to say, Mrs. Brown did say he looked quite dashing in his uniform."

"What else did Mrs. Brown say?" Ali asked cautiously.

"She said he seemed quite nice."

"He is," Ali agreed, cutting the chicken with her fork.

"But she said you seemed a little bothered. Was something wrong?"

"No, nothing was wrong. We met for dinner after work."

Tess patted her daughter's arm. "Did you have a bad day?"

"No," Ali replied, her knife cutting faster. "But I did have to be Bundles at school."

"Aw, and the head ruined your hair. Is that why you were upset?" Somer asked.

"Who said I was upset?" Ali asked. "I had a good day. The kids loved me."

"Then why did you close the curtains in the cozy?" Trent asked, not wanting his sister to get off that easy.

Ali slowly turned her head to her brother. "If you must know, it was because Telebrown and Tattlemeyers made sure they got a table at the restaurant right in front of us, and I didn't feel like being watched all the way through dinner."

Tess began to nod. "I can understand that. There's nothing worse than someone watching you eat."

Ali glowered at her brother. "Thanks, Mom."

"So unless you want the three of us to stare at you

until you're ready to talk, I think you might want to tell us about your dinner last night."

Ali snapped her head around. "You wouldn't."

"We would," Somer cut in. "You didn't just start living with us. You know better. We're Archers. We do what we have to do in order to get what we want. You know that."

Ali certainly did know that. She had employed the technique many times, most recently getting Jake to help her get a drum set out of that car's trunk, a simple act that had begun the countdown to this Armageddon. Besides, she was outnumbered. "As I said, we met for dinner."

"Jake met you in uniform, and you wore your penguin suit?" Trent asked, his voice more quizzical than humorous. "Aren't women afraid of getting their hair all messed up before a date?"

"It wasn't a date," Ali quickly said.

"You went to dinner. It was a date."

Ali swiveled to fully face her brother. "No, it wasn't."

"What was it, then?" Trent returned quickly.

"It's a little complicated."

"You have our attention," Trent said with a grin. "Linda is at class, and Nick is at the pistol range at target practice because he has to qualify again soon, so we have all night if you need it."

"Have some meatloaf with your chicken, Ali," Tess suggested, cutting off a healthy piece from the loaf.

"Somer says estrogen blocks the truth serum in that stuff, Mom," Trent said. "It won't work on her."

"I've changed the recipe," Tess assured him. "And Ali could use more protein in her diet." She slid the meatloaf onto Ali's plate.

"Don't eat anything before I can have the forensics labs run some tests on it," Trent warned his baby sister.

"All your fancy tests will say is that there's some ground round, eggs, bread crumbs, salt, pepper, onions, and ketchup in it," Tess assured.

"It's the ketchup," Trent said, eyeing the red bottle suspiciously. "Let's get Leonard the Rocket Scientist over here. He figured out the love connection to the brain thing, so maybe he can figure out what chemical reaction happens when ketchup is added to meatloaf and then cooked at three hundred fifty degrees." He narrowed his eyes at his mother. "Mom did take that exotic cooking class when she went to Thailand last year."

Tess laughed. "There is nothing special in the meatloaf." To prove it she took a big bite of the slice she had on her own plate, chewed and swallowed it. "See, it's nothing. There's no foaming at the mouth, no glazing of the eyes, no trance. Ali will share with us what happened at dinner with Jake because she wants to share it with us, that's all."

"That and to make sure the real story goes around town a hundred times, and not let the resident gossips write one for their own enjoyment."

Ali knew she had no choice. Her mom was right. She either told her family what happened, or rather what did not happen at the restaurant, or Mrs. Brown and Mrs. Meyers would tell everyone for her, complete with a racy ending, no doubt. She'd tell them, but she would blame it on the meatloaf—for tradition's sake.

"When I got to the school, Jake was already there. A

little boy named Billy asked him to come and talk to his class dressed like a soldier."

"That's a pretty unique show-and-tell," Trent said.

"Jake's a war hero," Ali said quickly.

"We didn't know you knew that, dear," Tess said.

"Or that you cared," Somer said.

"What's that supposed to mean?" Ali asked her sister.

Somer ignored her sister's glower. "I just thought you were too busy at work making park benches out of plastic laundry containers to notice much of anything else."

"I don't make park benches out of plastic laundry containers," Ali corrected. "I make sure that the people understand about recycling enough not to throw them in the trash stream so other people can make the park benches. It saves the planet and helps the economy." Ali pushed herself back in the chair with insincere insight. "Oh, that's right, sister darling, you don't work anymore." She pasted on her sweetest fake smile. "And how are things on *Jerry Springer* these days?"

Tess tapped her fork on her plate. "You two, stop. If I wanted to listen to this bickering again, I would have never given you your grandmother's rings."

On cue, all three siblings turned to their mother, their mouths perfect O's.

"And now that I have your attention," Tess said to them. "I believe Ali was going to tell us about her dinner with Jake."

Trent and Somer had already gone home when Ali finished drying the large fryer skillet for her mother.

"Mom," she said, handing it to Tess, "when did you know Dad was the one?"

"Why do you ask, dear?"

Ali coughed and rubbed her nose. "I just wondered."

Tess took the dishtowel from Ali's hand and pulled out a kitchen chair from its place at the table. "Sit down."

Ali took a careful breath and complied. Tess sat next to her.

"I was eighteen when I met your father," Tess began. "It was at a concert. The band was called America."

"Is that why you always sang us to sleep with the song 'A Horse with No Name' instead of a normal lullaby?"

"It could be," Tess said with a wink. "I thought your father was the handsomest man I ever saw." She looked off into the distance as she remembered. "His hair came to his shoulders, and he parted it in the middle. I remember thinking it was the color of a field of wheat when the sun hit it. I couldn't see his eyes at first. He wore round, dark glasses, the wire kind with no rims, just like John Lennon. He had on a denim shirt over a tee shirt, with dark blue denim bell-bottomed jeans." She looked back at Ali. "He was tall and thin. When he started to walk over to me with his hands in his pockets, my heart started beating like a tom-tom."

Ali thought she could see it all happening over again in her mother's eyes. "Then what happened?"

"Well, when he got to me, he didn't say a word. He just looked at me with that great big smile of his for what seemed like hours. Then he took one hand out of his pocket and tucked my hair behind my ears. At the time, my hair was long and straight and blond. Come to think of it, it looked a lot like his, only mine came down almost to my waist."

"Mom," Ali said in a whiney voice, dragging out the word, "what did he *say* to you?"

Tess smiled. "He picked up his sunglasses with his other hand and said, 'There, now I can see your beautiful eyes.' And that's when I saw his. They were the lightest shade of blue I had ever seen on a man, almost silver. When he looked at me that day, I thought I could see all the way down to his soul. Then the concert started and we didn't talk again until it was over."

"That didn't tell me very much."

"Then maybe you should let me finish."

Ali nodded her agreement.

"After the concert, we walked to the park about a block away and stayed there talking until the sun came up over the lake. At lot of other couples ended up in the park, too, but they did a lot more than just talk. You know the era." She held up her fingers in a vee in the instantly recognizable symbol of her generation. "Peace and love, and especially free love, was what it was all about. But not your father. He was a perfect gentleman."

"Dad was always a special person," Ali agreed.

"I think that's when I knew we were going to be to-gether." Tess's eyes filled with loving tears. "And we had a wonderful life from that day on."

Ali reached out and took her mother's hand. "I miss him, too, Mom."

Tess took the dishtowel she'd been holding and dabbed at her eyes. "You know it when you know it, when you meet the one who is right for you. It could be in an hour, a day, a week, or a year." She patted her daughter's hand and looked into her eyes. "I can't explain it. You just know he's the one."

Back home in bed in her town house, Ali couldn't sleep. The entire conversation she had with her mother ran through her head and her heart like ticker tape.

Why did Jake affect her so?

Did she know why?

More important, what else did she know?

That he was her *one*?

She ran her hands through her hair to try to massage out a building headache. That was a silly notion. No matter what her mother said, no one finds their other half in less than a week.

She reached for the light to turn it off when her cell phone on the nightstand pinged with an incoming text message. She bolted to a sitting position and opened it.

"R U still awake?"

She didn't recognize the number.

"Who is this?" she texted back.

"Guess," came the instant reply.

"Is it u, Jake?"

"Yes it's Jake."

"Whose phone is this?"

"It's mine. It's reloadable."

A warmth spread through her. She knew he'd gotten it for her. *"I was just thinking about you. Where R U?"* she asked him.

"I'm in Hoboken. But I'd rather be with U. R U free Saturday?"

She couldn't answer him fast enough. *"Yes I am."*

"Can we go out?"

"Yes as long as it is not within 25 miles of Hillsborough."

"Y is that?"

"I'll explain when you pick me up."

"See U Saturday at 8."

"I'll be ready."

She looked at the screen for a while and then turned off the phone. Now she could sleep.

Chapter Eleven

The doorbell rang at exactly 8:00 P.M. Even though she knew he'd be on time, Ali felt a warm rush of anticipation run through her as soon as she heard it.

They'd heated up the airways texting each other over the last few days, possibly even melting a cell tower of two. But it really couldn't be helped. She had gone beyond being interested and curious about Jake, and was quickly moving into the region of "need to know."

She needed to know whether all the slow looks she kept catching him give when they were together meant what she thought they meant. She needed to know if they would keep in touch when he want back overseas, or whether she was a pursuit of the moment. She needed to know that, if she wasn't, what she felt for him could stand the tests of time and distance.

And most of all she needed to know why, in just knowing him for a week, she needed to know so much about him.

She sighed. She really needed to know.

She pulled the door open as if her life depended on it, and tried not to look like it. But if what she was feeling in her heart showed up on her face when their gazes locked, she knew she wouldn't be fooling anyone.

He looked great. With a light blue shirt tucked into dark indigo jeans, there was no question about the toned and tapered body they covered. The slight breeze in the October air sent the pleasing scent of citrus from his skin to her nostrils. His eyes were lit with the pleasure of seeing her again, and the smile on his lips was just big enough to emphasize his great mouth.

How she did not throw herself into his arms, she did not know.

"Hi," she said instead, gripping the edge of the door to keep from acting on what every part of her was telling her to do.

He held out a bunch of flowers. "Hi to you, too."

She took them from his hand and gestured for him to come inside. "If you think bringing me flowers is going to rack you up any brownie points, you can forget it," she said with a laugh. She walked to the kitchen with Jake following close behind.

He stopped in the doorway and leaned against it, watching her reach for a tall vase from inside one of the cabinets. "I wasn't going for the brownie points."

"So you are learning a little." She put the vase under the faucet and turned on the water. While it filled, she freed the flowers from their cellophane casing.

"Actually, I stopped at a grocery store on the way here to get some soda, and the Girl Scouts were selling flowers as a fund raiser for the troops for Operation New Jersey Cares. I thought it would help send some socks over to some of the guys I know back at the base. A few could use some more than others," he said with a laugh.

Ali put the flowers in the water and spun to face him. "I do understand. Socks are important." He could see a flash of disappointment on her face.

"Gotcha," he said in response. "I did buy them for you. So what do you say? Ten brownie points."

She wrinkled her nose. "Five—I'm taking off five for your tricking me."

He walked to her and put his hands on her waist. "What do five brownie points get a guy these days?"

She looked up into his incredible eyes and almost told him he could have whatever he wanted. "A kiss on the cheek," she said instead.

Jake touched her cheek with his forefinger and then moved it across her cheek to her lips. "How many points would it take to move the target a few inches?"

"A lot more than five," Ali said, her voice coming in a whisper.

Jake smiled and took a step back. "The night is young, so then I think I'll bank the five I have for the moment."

He walked her to a metallic green Mercury Marquis parked in the driveway.

"Is it rented?" Ali asked.

"No, it's mine. It resides at Mom's until I get back stateside. And she says 'hi,' by the way."

"Hi to her," Ali said walking to the passenger-side

door and waiting until Jake opened it for her before sliding into the leather seat. She watched Jake jog easily around the car and settle into the driver's side.

"Where are we going?" Ali asked him.

"I'm taking you to one of my favorite clubs down the shore near the Air Force Base. It's called Arian's. Have you ever heard of it?"

Ali nodded. "It's supposed to have great food and good club bands."

"And it has good dancing," Jake added.

Ali leaned back. "You dance?"

"When I'm not flying, dodging tracers, or getting shot at by some fanatic, I like to kick up my heels, now and then." He saw Ali's face pale. "I mean, when I'm done with the mission for the day, I go to the O Club to decompress. The nurses over there love to dance. So it helps us all relax."

Ali cut her eyes to him. "I'll just bet it does."

"Don't be so skeptical. It's good fun and a way to get away from the war for a while."

"I told you. I've seen *M*A*S*H* a thousand times, and I have a vision that instead of Hawaiian shirts, you guys wear one of those long white shirt-thing robes and drink homemade hooch out of one of those things that looks like a baker's hat."

"I'm afraid it wouldn't hold very much hooch." Jake eased the car onto Route One near Trenton, heading toward McGuire Air Force Base.

"Okay, I'll give you that point, but I'm sure then you learned your dancing technique by charming all the Iraqi women there."

Jake blew out a long breath of air and shook his head. "I see you haven't read much on the subject. That's one thing we would *never* do. It could cost an innocent lady her life to be seen that close to one of us. The family of a woman in the Middle East is very serious about protecting her from us infidels."

"I think I did hear something about that."

"The Arab Iraqi women's clothes are designed to conceal them. And we wouldn't think of putting them in any danger by trying to make them. So you can say dancing is out."

"I guess the nurses get really tired feet then, from having to dance with the whole squad," Ali quipped.

"They serve their country with pride and dignity."

"Hmm," Ali said, crossing her arms over her chest. "Where did I hear that one before?"

Jake looked at her and winked. "Packages from home are nice, but once in a while you really need to talk to a lady, if only to remember what you are really fighting for."

"And that would be?"

"That would be family, country, and freedom." He looked down at her lips and then back into her eyes. "And don't forget love."

Jake turned his attention back to the road and Ali felt the warm current flow through her again. She let everything Jake told her sink in for the next few miles. She'd never thought much about freedom, and had to admit she was a bit embarrassed for taking it for granted. She'd never do that again, she promised herself.

A car pulled out from a parking slot three spaces down

from the club and Jake guided his car into the open space.

"Someone's watching over you," Ali teased.

Jake's eyes cut to the sky for the slightest fraction of a second. "I certainly hope so." He got out, jogged around the front of the car and opened the passenger door. "Shall we?" he asked, holding out his hand.

"Why not?" Ali said, taking it. He didn't let her hand go when he closed the door and pressed the automatic lock, and she didn't try to pull it free.

The music that could be heard from the parking lot got louder when they opened the door to the club. Inside, it seemed to vibrate with life, shaking from floor to ceiling with noise, voices and busy feet. The band played against the far wall, and the music was so deafening that Ali could barely hear her own thoughts.

Holding on tightly to her hand and pulling her with him, Jake snaked his way through the bodies moving in time to the music, acknowledging people with a nod or a smile. He found a small table off to one side. The patrons before them had apparently just left because the tabletop was still sticky. A bleached blond waitress wiped it down for them.

"What're you gonna have?" she asked, tucking the dishrag into the back pocket of her skin-tight jeans.

Jake looked at Ali, waiting for her to order. "I'll have a club soda with lemon," she shouted over the run of a guitar solo.

"Make mine the same," Jake said, putting up two fingers to make sure the waitress knew he was going to stick with the harmless drink too.

Ali looked around. Everyone seemed to know everyone. Or else they knew each other well enough to dance and change partners whenever the mood struck. The dance floor was so crowded that Ali couldn't tell who was with whom. Lights flashed, voices echoed, and no one seemed to have a care in the world.

"Is this where you come when you're home on leave?" Ali asked. She had to lean over and practically shout in his ear in order to make sure he heard her.

"I come here when I feel like getting away for a few hours," he acknowledged.

"It seems like you know a lot people here," Ali said as a short dark-haired man with a blond wrapped all over him shouted a greeting to Jake.

Jake scooted his chair around to get closer to her. "I don't know as many as you might think. I've been out of the country for over a year. Most of the people I knew are gone, and the ones left are probably in transit one way or the other."

Ali nodded, a little uncomfortable being out of her comfort zone and in his.

"How do you like the band?" he asked her.

She was glad he had moved closer. "It's definitely not soft pop."

"It's a local group, a down-and-dirty rock band from Trenton. I like that type of music once in a while. What do you think?"

Ali struggled with tuning into the hard, pulsating music and repetitive lyrics. Over the driving rhythm, the lead singer was shouting something about what he did the night before and with whom.

"I think the lead singer is going to be hoarse by the end of the night," she said.

Jake laughed and grabbed her hand. "Dance with me."

She looked out onto the packed dance floor. "I'm not sure there's room for us."

"C'mon, we can at least find a space to start moving."

Ali looked out at the mass of bodies. "If we do, I can think of a few Commandments we're going to break in the process."

"Which ones?"

Looking around, she saw several young men laughing and changing partners. "Looks like 'thou shall not covet,' to start with."

Jake's laugh grew heartier right before he pulled her toward the dance floor, snaking his way around tables and bumping into people along the way. She lost count of the number of feet they stepped on.

"Jake, maybe it would be better if we just watched until the dance floor clears a little."

He shook his head. "No, it would be better if we danced. Put your arms around me so we don't get separated." He slipped his arms around her waist and held her close.

When they settled into a rhythm, his face was close to hers. The heat from his body seemed like a furnace. The air was thick with the scent of liquor and competing perfumes, but she didn't care. As her head filled with the backbeat of the music, her senses tuned into Jake's strong male essence. The heat of his body made the citrus of his aftershave rise on his skin. She closed her eyes and inhaled. It was a scent she would remember for a long time.

The beat of the music slowed and she felt his body adjust. She swayed with him, enjoying the feel of his arm around her.

"This makes no sense," she said, lifting her head and looking into his eyes.

"It makes perfect sense to me," he said, spinning her around as much as the crowd around them would allow before pulling her back into his arms with such a casual grace that it made her nod her approval of the move. "It's a great club. It can be sweet, or satisfying, or just plain fun."

Her hands braced on his shoulders; she moved her face closer to his. "It's not the club that doesn't make sense. It's us."

"I know," he acknowledged. "But, for now, let's let it just be fun." He spun her in two fast circles as the song ramped the music up, he eyes lighting with amusement when she laughed before he pulled her back into his arms.

She caught her breath when her body rammed into his. "Where did you learn to do that?" His smile seemed to stop her heart for a moment. "I thought all soldiers were only adept at marching, not dancing."

"In between airlifts, we have to find something to do."

"So you dance with each other? Just the sight of it must scare the heck out of the enemy."

Jake threw back his head and laughed. "That could end the war, all right. Actually, back in the eighth grade, I had a gym teacher who conspired with the girl's gym teacher to make us all do ballroom dancing. It was the most painful semester I ever spent."

"That's cruel," Ali said. "I can just imagine how that must have been to a roomful of pre-teens who were just beginning to figure out what's going on. It must have felt pretty awkward."

He made sure he caught her gaze full-on. "I can tell you it never felt like this."

The intensity of his gaze made her miss a step. Jake's arms tightened around her to keep her from falling. As if on cue, the volume of the music eased down and the beat slowed.

"I think this one will stay slow," Jake said in response. "Now what you have to do is drape yourself all over me and we won't have to worry about injuries for a while."

"I think I already am," Ali acknowledged.

"But I think we can get closer." His hands moved low on her hips.

"Jake," Ali whispered. "I think we're starting to break another Commandment."

"I agree, and it's one of my personal favorites."

The music turned soft and mesmerizing, the room seeming to heat to boiling as the couples dancing got closer to each other.

"This may not be a good idea," Ali murmured as her cheek pressed against Jake's.

She thought her voice was just a whisper, but he heard

her. "It's a great idea, so let's be a little reckless, if only for a little while."

"But it's not going to last—you're going . . ."

"Shh," he said, interrupting her. "It can last as long as we want it to last." He kissed her forehead. "It can last as long as you would like."

She closed her eyes as his lips touched her skin. Forever—she wanted it to last forever.

Without warning, she felt his lips swoop down on hers. Her reaction was swift and sudden. She rose on her toes to press her lips more fully to his. The connection to him sent a shock right down to her toes. The need to keep kissing him bubbled inside her until it almost became a living part of her.

And it scared her. This wasn't like her at all. She'd never felt anything this sudden and this intense. She didn't believe in love at first sight, and certainly she didn't believe in love in a week.

She broke away from him. "I need to powder my nose." It was an old line, but the only one she could think of at the moment.

She moved quickly away from him and he let her go, watching as the crowd seemed to gobble her up.

Chapter Twelve

The ladies' room was nearly as packed as the dance floor. Women primped at the mirrors, either talking about the men in the club or complaining about other women. The room reeked of perfume and sweat.

Ali found a spot at the far sink and ran the cold water. She splashed some of it on her face. She raised her head and looked at herself in the spotty mirror. Her heart beat a furious rhythm against her chest. She touched a finger to her lips. They were still warm from Jake's kiss. She gripped the sides of the sink hard to stop herself from running back into his arms.

The feelings she had for him were all so new to her that they frightened her. None of it felt like her, yet all of it felt right. She just didn't know how it was going to fit into her life, *if* it would fit into her life. That's what scared her the most.

Why did she have these strong feelings for someone she hardly knew? Could it be more than the sudden rush of something new, and exciting, and safe? Was she throwing caution to the wind because she knew Jake would be leaving soon?

She looked around the room. It seemed like none of the other women were stressing as much as she was. None of them seemed the least bit worried at all. They would probably go back out and dance, and then go home with someone or go home alone. To them, it didn't seem to matter. In the morning, their lives would go on as though nothing had ever happened.

But she wasn't like any of them. She needed to know what she was doing and what she was feeling. Casual dating and playful flirting were not her style.

Get a grip, Ali, she told herself, *and think. It's all just the excitement of the evening—or hero-worship.* After all, Jake was a handsome war hero. He was a darned attractive soldier. The memory of him in uniform was something she would never forget.

That had to be it, she decided. It couldn't be anything more. The world wasn't the same as it had been when her mother had fallen head over heels with her father in a matter of thirty-six seconds back in the late sixties. Life was more complicated now. People took their time now.

She took a deep breath and walked back into the club. She bumped and jostled herself in the direction of the table where they had begun the evening. Along the way, one guy offered to buy her a drink. Another grabbed her hand and wanted her to dance with him. She pulled her hand free only to have someone else grab her arm. She turned, fire-ready to give the person a piece of her mind when she saw it was Jake.

"I should have brought you to a better club," he said, steering her toward the door. "This was a bad idea."

"No, it wasn't really." She looked around the crowded room on her way out. "Maybe just the club part wasn't the greatest idea. But we still have the beach and the ocean. Why don't we get some air and enjoy that view?"

He nodded and took her hand. She let him lead the way out the door and down an old boardwalk that led to the sand. A few feet down on the beach they settled onto a bench seat facing the water. For a while, neither one spoke. They sat quietly and looked out at the waves rolling onto the beach. The moonlight painted a silver hue onto the light tones of the vista. The contrast against the darkness of the night that colored the ocean to what seemed a deep navy blue made the mood almost hypnotic.

"I guess I came on a bit strong," Jake confessed to her after a new minutes.

Ali leaned back, stretching her legs out so her body was reclined on the bench. "I think I'm actually flattered in a way." Jake seemed to relax when he heard that.

"You're being more than kind."

"No, I mean it. You are a handsome man."

His head cocked. "You think I'm handsome."

She sat up and angled her body to him. "I do. And so do many of the beautiful women in that club. I noticed heads turn when you danced by a few."

"I hadn't noticed."

Ali smiled. "I know, and that's why I'm flattered. You weren't looking at anyone but me. I'll bet they were all jealous of me. We are one heck of a couple, you know."

Her words appeared to render Jake speechless because he only smiled and looked out over the water.

"Did I say something wrong?" Ali asked after what seemed to her to be a long stretch of silence.

He shook his head, but stared straight ahead.

"Something's wrong," she pressed.

He turned back to her. "It's nothing."

A shiver ran up Ali's spine. She didn't know if it had come from the cool breeze blowing off the water or the sadness she saw in Jake's eyes. "Maybe this was a bad idea."

She started to get up but Jake stopped her with a hand to her arm. "It's not you. It's me."

A nervous laugh bubbled out of her. "How many times have I heard that one? It's a good thing we didn't register at Macy's."

"What do you mean?"

"Those are break-up words. You're about to tell me that the past few days have been fun, but we should just go our separate ways. I recognize the phrasing."

"That's not even close," he said, pulling her against him so her back rested against his chest. He looped his arm around her, his hand resting on her forearm.

"Then what is it?" she asked, staring out at the horizon, afraid if she turned and looked at him, he would see something in her eyes that she wasn't ready to reveal just yet.

His fingers gently massaged her arm. "Oh, I don't know, Ali. It's a lot of things."

She swallowed hard, unsure of what was coming next.

"Before I left for Iraq, I thought I knew everything there was to know about life. But being over there"—he blew out another breath and then kissed the top of her head—"I just don't know what to think."

She turned in his arms. It was easy to see the discomfort on his face, his unhappiness with his turmoil. She hated knowing that she put it there. "I'm so sorry, Jake. You don't have to tell me anything."

"Yes I do." He unwound his arm from around her, but kept his eyes on her. "There was this girl. About six months before I shipped out, I met her. I knew I was going away sometime, but I just didn't know when. We latched onto each other like barbed wire."

Ali blinked, her heart racing. What was he going to tell her? Maybe she didn't want to know.

"Oh," she said in a small voice, biting down on her lip. "I think I get the picture. There's no need to go into it any further."

"We were good together," he continued, ignoring her, "right up until the day I left."

Ali felt her lip begin to quiver. Didn't he know he was killing her? She didn't want to know about him with another woman. She couldn't bear the thought of someone else in his arms.

She put a hand to his chest and pushed against it. "Jake, please stop."

He covered her hand with hers and would not let it go. "No, I need you to understand. It was all heat and no heart. We just didn't care much except about the here and now. That's what it came down to. The day I left for Iraq, it was over. I knew it. She knew it. There was no other man, no other woman. It just stopped."

Ali dipped her head. "Did you love her?"

Jake's free hand caught her chin with his fingertips and brought it up so his gaze could meet hers. "No, I didn't. And she didn't love me. And neither one of us cared enough to work too hard on that part of the relationship."

To Ali the answer was sad and much worse than if he had said that he had loved her. "You deserve better," she said softly.

"So did she," he admitted.

The sadness was back in his eyes and she knew she had to ask the question again. "Are you sure you didn't love her, Jake?"

His retuning smile erased some of the melancholy from the lines of his face. "I'm sure. You can forget a lot of things in life, but you can't forget love. And that's the one thing I don't remember when I think back on the relationship."

"Maybe you're just blocking the feeling. There was so much going on then—your going overseas, the violence there, the fear that you might not come home."

"That wasn't it at all. The fighting, the fear, all of it came with the territory. I knew that when I took the job. We used each other, Ali. We wanted fun and good times, and just didn't care about anything permanent."

Ali wrenched her hand free and stood. The evening had started as enjoyable but was now ending on a miserable note. And it was all her fault. When she looked down at Jake, she thought she could see both anger and fear in his eyes.

"Maybe we should go home," she whispered.

"We can't go just yet," he said, standing. "Now there's something I need to know."

Holding his gaze, Ali nodded.

"If you loved someone, if someone was important to you, even if you knew he could be gone in a heartbeat, would you ever forget what you had with him, even if it was only for a little while?"

She closed her eyes against the building tears. The last few minutes seemed to have developed a life of their own, and reached right into her chest and squeezed her heart. She didn't know how to answer him, didn't know the right thing to say. When his fingers brushed the side of her face, she opened her eyes.

"You wouldn't forget," she answered him, "if it mattered."

Without warning, his mouth crushed hers, pressing the backs of her legs against the bench, nearly knocking her off balance. His kisses battered them with both frustration and need. Gone were the patience and the slow dance of dating. What was left was the raw need that bubbled beneath it.

In his kiss came the need for something more, something permanent and committing.

And then came the panic.

The reality of the short time she'd known him snagged the air from her throat. She simply wasn't prepared or equipped to promise that she was any different from the girl who left him the first time. It was too soon to promise him that this time would be different. What if he did go away, and time proved that she could forget him and the time they spent together? What if it did the same for him?

Her heartbeat rose, and she knew it wasn't because he was kissing her. It was the reality of their situation setting in.

If she did anything to hurt him and something happened to him over his deployment, she could never forgive herself. Maybe it would be better if he wasn't distracted on his missions by someone waiting for him at home. She didn't know what to do. She just didn't know.

So she pushed him away and stepped back. She hugged her arms over her chest in a defensive move she knew he would understand.

And he let her go, looking at her like a deer caught in the headlights

"I'm sorry, Jake. This is all happening a bit too fast."

He lifted his hands, palms out. "It's my problem, not yours. I'll take you home."

After he took her home, he circled around the block and parked on the street a house away from hers so he could see the light in her window.

It wasn't so much examining his own life that set him off. He knew the highs and lows he'd experienced over the last year. He knew the triumphs and the mistakes.

It was the fact that he thought he'd met the woman with whom he could spend the rest of his life. He only had about three weeks left to convince her that he was sure of it, that it wasn't like the last time he had deployed.

Why on earth had he told her about the last time anyway? This was nothing like the last time. He could remember every minute he spent with Ali and he always would.

He wanted love, and he wanted it with Ali. He didn't care if he'd known her for one day, one week, one year, or one minute. He knew it was right. She was his match, his equal, and he wanted her to tumble into love with him as completely as he had tumbled into love with her.

It wasn't reasonable, but then, neither was love. There is never a reason for being in love—you simply are.

He looked up at her window just as the light went out.

"Sweet dreams, honey," he whispered, "and sleep well. Our adventure is just beginning."

Chapter Thirteen

Ali rose early the next day. As she brushed her teeth in preparation to go to work, she looked at herself in the mirror. She'd changed and she knew it. Jake had seen to that.

He'd hit her life like a sudden summer storm—rapid, intense, unpredictable. Just like a storm rolls across the landscape changing it, Jake had changed everything she thought she knew.

But the sudden shift in his mood last night had left her baffled. He moved between melancholy and intense so quickly that it upset her. Now she wondered if she knew anything at all, especially anything about men like Jake.

Men like Jake—the phrase ran through her mind over and over like ticker tape as she rinsed and put away her toothbrush. Exactly who was Jake Daultry anyway?

Was he a man who could shift moods quickly all the time? And if he was, could a woman like her handle him?

Should she be cool and remote until he explained himself further? Or should she be casual and warm, and ignore the whole thing?

She knew she couldn't ignore the way he kissed her as though he couldn't get enough. Neither could she discount how closely they'd danced, as if they were being fused by the heat of the moment. And there was no way to discount the way she felt about him.

None of that was possible, not after last night. Now her mood shifted from questioning to annoyed as she ripped open her closet and chose a print shirt and black slacks. How on earth was she supposed to know how to act around him? She had no idea if he'd ever kissed anyone like that before, no idea if he felt the way she was feeling now.

Just because she was falling in love with him, was she supposed to meekly go in whatever direction Jake wanted her to go?

Her eyes widened. What had she just thought? Of course she wasn't falling in love with him. She didn't fall in love with men after just a week.

She slammed her insulated travel mug onto the countertop and poured the coffee that had been made automatically while she was in the shower. Whatever she was feeling, it couldn't be love.

Maybe her mother fell in love with her father five minutes after she met him. Maybe Somer could fall in love with Nick in just under ten minutes. Maybe even Trent could find Linda at Somer and Nick's wedding.

But that wasn't her. She might be spontaneous. She

might be impetuous. But she wasn't a fool. She wasn't going to be the second girl he forgot after he deployed. She wanted the heart not the heat, and she would settle for nothing less.

"Are you having man trouble?" Diana paused at Ali's desk on her way to her cubicle.

"Is it that obvious?" Ali asked her.

"I could hear you smashing the keyboard keys from the hallway. What's up?"

Ali's shoulders shrugged. "Nothing's wrong that a mind reader couldn't fix."

Diana perched her backside on the edge of Ali's desk. "Yeah, we could all use a dose of that once in a while." She tapped her finger on her chin. "Who is that mind-reading hunk in *Heroes?*"

"His name's Matt Parkman," Ali answered.

"Yeah, Matt Parkman, that's it. And he can place ideas in your mind. Can you imagine what a girl could do with a power like that?"

"Save the world," Ali said, flatly.

"No, save us from them. We could finally figure out what makes an alpha-male tick." She rose and shifted her shoulder bag onto the other shoulder. "Besides which, we could figure out how to get them to replace the toilet paper and take out the garbage."

"That is the least of my worries," Ali groaned.

"Then what I'm about to say isn't going to help."

Ali eyed Diana suspiciously. "Don't tell me I have to spend more time in the penguin suit."

"No, it's worse than that."

"What could possibly be worse then prancing around in a felt oven feeling your hair soak up every ounce of perspiration you can generate?"

"How about doing it for a whole weekend at Green Fest?"

"You are kidding me." Ali tried not to glare at her boss, but it was becoming more difficult by the moment as she pictured herself with flippers again.

Diana shook her head. "You have to cover. Melissa has a medical emergency and will be out for three weeks." She dug into her bag and pulled out the flyer. "You know the county is pulling out all the stops on the 'Go-Green' thing this year."

Ali reluctantly took the flyer. "I don't suppose there is anything I can do to get out of this."

"Nope, sorry, there's not. Rank has its privileges. I covered Earth Day in April. You have to cover Green Fest in October. Besides, it could be fun."

Ali glanced at the flyer and then back at Diana. "How do you think?"

"It's at the Garden State Convention Center. It's just three days, you'll meet lots of people, and they'll think you're a penguin." Diana's expression stayed serious for about two minutes before she lost it and burst out laughing. "Maybe you'll meet a walrus," she said as she walked away.

"Oh, that's very funny. You owe me," Ali called out.

"Meet a walrus," she heard Diana say to another co-worker before they both broke into laughter.

"Laugh it up," Ali mumbled. "You are going to want

something from me one of these days, and you know what they say about payback."

A loud ping suddenly came from Ali's purse telling her there was a text message. She knew it was from Jake before she opened it.

"Can U talk?"

She hesitated answering, wondering what he wanted to talk about. What she didn't need was more information to coil around what she was already fighting. She started to put the cell phone back in its place in the inside pocket of her purse, but found herself replying instead. Jake was much too much a part of her life for her to simply ignore.

"Not really," she texted back. *"Y talk now?"*

"Because I owe you an apology. Can we hook up?"

The thought of seeing him kicked her heartbeat up a notch. It led her to wonder again what it was about him that made her so anxious. A woman in this millennium was no doe-eyed maiden who needed to jump whenever a man asked.

But she'd never met anyone like Jake who had her falling so far and so fast into uncharted territory of the heart. So she'd kissed him a few times. From the spontaneity of the first time to the deliberateness of the last one, kissing Jake was a purely feminine reaction. It was what a woman does when she knows a man is attracted to her. So she agreed to meet him.

"Sure, see U at 5, after work?" She typed in.

"Where?" was the question back.

"See U at Maggie's, a deli in Hillsborough."

"I'll find it on my GPS. See you there."

She flipped the phone closed and put it away. Okay, they'd talk and eat a sandwich. What harm could that do?

By four she found herself doing what she never thought she'd do: clock watching. Diana caught her.

"You in a hurry to be somewhere?" Diana asked.

"I just need to get the penguin suit to the cleaners before it closes."

"I doubt that. Green Fest is two weekends away," Diana replied, putting the latest recycling contracts into Ali's in-box. "I need you to go over the bid specs on these before you go home because I need a recommendation to award the contracts in the morning. You may have to stay late to do it."

"Shoot, I needed to get out on time today."

"Sorry, but it can't be helped. The commodities market is about to jump, and we have to be on it."

"You owe me big-time," Ali said.

Diana saluted her agreement and left.

Ali's hand floated over her purse. She should text Jake and tell him that she would be late. It would be the considerate thing to do. She dug around for her cell and found his number in her contact list. Her fingers flew across the keypad.

"I'm going 2 B late."

Almost as soon as she hit SEND, it seemed, a reply came.

"How late? I'm hungry."

She read the simple message and smiled. Thank you, cell company. She never imagined technology would make her feel so warm and wanted.

"You're just hungry?"

She knew she had baited him.

The response came immediately gain. *"I didn't say what for."*

She laughed as she replied. *"LOL, snack on some chips and I'll be done as soon as I can."*

But as soon as she pushed the SEND button, she felt a moment's pang of indecision. Their banter was fun, but by encouraging it, did she make him feel as though they had started something that could go long-term? Was she giving him the impression that she was becoming more involved with him and overstepping the place in which they really were? Where were they in his mind, besides just enjoying each other's company while knowing that he would be leaving very soon?

And why was she over-thinking a simple courtesy text message?

He replied to her text by saying that chips would have to do, and she left it at that and reached for the contracts on her desk. She had to get them out before she went anywhere, or risk costing the taxpayers thousands of dollars.

When she did join Jake for dinner, she'd be careful not to order any chips.

It was well after six by the time she had just finished, and she suddenly heard Jake's voice behind her say, "I wasn't going to let you stand me up."

She spun around and stared at him, her heartbeat up again just by looking at him. "You're going to make me have a heart attack some day," she said. The way her heart raced around him so much lately made her certain of it.

"I didn't mean to scare you."

"How did you get past security?"

"I told them I was your boyfriend."

"Did you now?"

"I did."

"And what did they say?"

"One of them said you were a lucky girl."

Ali gave him a knowing nod. "That must have been Pat."

Jake smiled in response. "I think that's what her ID said."

"Why did you come here?"

"You have to eat. When you weren't at the deli, I took a chance that you might have been held up at work." He held out a paper bag.

"You brought me food?"

"I brought food."

A quick glance at the sparkle in his eyes told her that he was quite impressed with himself. Her heart warmed. It was very thoughtful of him.

"What did you bring? Did you bring anything interesting?"

"That I did." A smile formed on his face, and he leaned toward her so that his nose almost touched hers. Then he tilted his head and focused his gaze on her parted lips. "Does the county have security cameras?" he asked her.

"It has a few. Why do you ask?"

"I'll just have to chance that none of them are pointed at your desk." He erased the distance between their lips. She was still for a moment and then relaxed, moving her lips in a soft brief touch that left her wanting more.

"We can't have any more kissing for a while," she said when she moved away.

"Why can't we?"

"It tends to distract me."

He brushed his finger over her lips. "But that's good."

Her laughter filled the air. "What's in the bag?"

Jake looked around her office. "Should we eat here?"

"Why not? It's quiet. It's private. We can talk."

Jake nodded as he opened the paper bag. "Hmm, *'talk'* sounds serious."

Watching him from her desk chair, Ali wondered about the mystery that was Jake Daultry. He did have her tied up in knots. She needed to untie a few before things went too much further. She cleared off a spot on her desk as he produced two sandwiches, some chips, and two cans of soda.

"Pull over a chair from the next office," she directed. "Do you do this for all your pretend girlfriends?"

"No," Jake called back, wrestling with an office chair, "I usually get them Chinese."

"You're very funny," she called back.

While she waited, she unwrapped the sandwiches from the white paper. She heard the chair roll in, but purposely avoided his eyes. She knew he had meant the comment as a joke, but it stole some of the glow she felt when he referred to himself as her boyfriend. Maybe that was a joke too.

"Do you approve?" he asked, sitting opposite her.

"It's fine," she replied fumbling with a packet of mayo. Okay, so he'd dated before—probably plenty. She knew that. He was an attractive man. But couple that with what she'd learned about the time before his last deployment, and it bothered her. It upset her too much, she admitted to herself. "I can't get this darn thing opened."

He reached over and took the packet from her, ripping it open in one fluid motion. "What's wrong?" he asked, handing it back.

"Nothing's wrong. It's just these stupid prepackaged condiments." She spread the mayo on her sandwich and took a bite so she wouldn't have to say any more.

He wasn't buying it. "I'm not a mind reader. You're going to have to tell me."

She suddenly felt like a schoolgirl eating lunch in the cafeteria across from the football hero. Every other time she knew where she stood with a guy she was interested in. She normally felt as though she had some measure of control, but not this time. Jake seemed to affect her more and more every day.

"I'm just being childish. Don't give it another thought."

"I don't think I can do that. I think a lot about you, Ali."

She could feel her cheeks warm and wondered how noticeable it was to Jake. "That's nice," she admitted.

"So, what is it then?"

She put down the sandwich and looked at him. Full speed ahead might be the best course of action. "I have to admit, this is a first for me."

"What, no one ever brought you food at work before?" His mouth quirked. "If no one has, then you've been seeing the wrong guys."

"And you're the right guy?"

He opened his sandwich. "Maybe I am."

Ali let the word hang in the air for a while, her heart beating hard. Could his *maybe* be a *yes?*

"What do you think?" he asked her over the silence.

"I think a lot of things, one of them that you don't really know me well."

"I know you."

"You don't know me well, and maybe don't know me well enough."

"I know you a lot better now than I did when I saw you bending over the bumper of your car trying to get a drum set out of your truck. I know how you laugh, how you kiss."

Jake saw Ali's cheeks blush fire-red. He loved it when he got that reaction from her. Not too many women he knew blushed anymore, certainly not any of them in the service. He liked that he had that physical reaction on Ali. It contrasted sharply with her sassy nature, letting him know she was interested.

"So let's talk more, then." He glanced around the office. "The security cameras don't have sound do they?"

She shook her head.

"Let's give it a try. You really don't know all that much about me except what you see on the outside and what you've gathered in the last few days."

"You could say the same thing about me."

"I know a lot. I'm a trained soldier. I need to gather information, process it, and made a decision quickly."

She slid her forearms onto her desk and leaned toward him. "So what do you think you know, hot shot?"

"I know your family. Or I sort of know them through what Nick has told me since he got married. I know what you do for a living, how you react to certain situations. I know there's a soft spot in your heart for children, and that you think the world can be saved by tossing glass into containers."

"My turn," she said. "You're a career soldier and a war hero. You like saving the world for democracy, but place a lower priority on the fact that what you're doing contributes to destroying the environment in the process. You like challenges, and you never back down from them. You don't compromise, don't settle for anything less than what you want." She lowered her eyes for a second and then looked back at him. "And you got hurt from your last relationship."

He swallowed and held up his hands in surrender. "I shouldn't have told you that. It's not who I am."

"I don't know why I brought that up," Ali confessed. "It's not my business."

There was a moment when she saw thoughts cross his eyes. Then a smile began at the corners of his lips, catching her attention. "I guess I'm going to have to find a way to make it your business."

Ali could feel the tension in her shoulders begin to dissipate. "And how are you going to do that?"

"I'll start by making myself so irresistible that you want to know every little detail about me."

She smiled, realizing there was no way for him to know that she already did. "I'm thinking, then, maybe you do need to start gathering some more brownie points."

"If I do, is there a list for me to cash them in?" He saw her smile as if a list had already formed in her mind. It made him happy to see her eyes sparkle with enthusiasm. He had a sudden desire to keep that look on her face as much as possible. Maybe in the short time he had left, he could even make her forget about the "other" woman.

"I almost forgot," he said digging into his shirt pocket. "There's an air show in two weeks on Saturday at McGuire Air Force Base. I thought we could go and I could show you my ride."

"What do you mean *your ride?*"

"There are a few Black Hawks in for repairs. I thought you might like to see one up close and personal."

"I would," Ali said, taking one of the tickets from him. She looked at the date. "But I'm working then."

"You're working on a Saturday?"

She nodded. "We save the planet 24-7-365. This morning my boss told me I have to work Green Fest at the Garden State Convention Center that weekend."

"What is Green Fest?"

"It's an eco-thing." Her face brightened. "Maybe you can come and learn."

"Will you be wearing the penguin suit?"

"I may."

"It is tempting, but I already volunteered to help out at the show."

Ali sighed. "I guess we won't be spending much time together that weekend."

"And I deploy the next."

"It's already coming so soon?" Ali hoped her voice didn't sound as anxious as she felt. Four weeks was flying by as if it were four minutes. She managed a weak smile. "Why do you have to go?" she whispered.

She looked away from him but not fast enough for him not to see her eyes shimmer. He went to her and pulled her to standing, wrapping an arm around her waist so she could not turn away. "It's what I do. I know you understand that."

"I never said that I didn't."

"Then let's enjoy the time we have left together."

His words felt like a rock inside her heart. She lowered her chin and bit down on her lip.

"Tell me what you're thinking, Ali."

She looked up at him. He was so tall, so muscled that she felt small and defenseless in his arms. It was a nice sensation, a sharp contrast to her always trying to be in control and on her game. For a moment she thought about just getting lost in his arms and forgetting about his leaving, but her mind wouldn't shut that out.

"What do you want from me?" she asked him. She felt his muscles flex and then his body still.

"I want you to give us a try."

"Why?" she whispered.

"I care about you."

To her it sounded as though he had to force out the words, and it worried her. "I don't know if I can, Jake."

"That's right, you can't know, and there's only one way you can find out, isn't there?"

Chapter Fourteen

Two weeks later, sitting in the back seat of a cab entering his last week on American soil, Jake was still asking himself why it found it so hard to tell Ali exactly how he felt about her. He thought he knew that almost from the first day he met her.

He was in love with her.

But she was wary about him and it was all his fault. He'd told her about the last time he was about to leave for Iraq. He just dropped it on her a like a bomb, with no warning, no explanation. How could he expect her to think this time would be different?

The last few weeks, they'd spent every minute they could together. And when that hadn't been possible, they'd heated up the airwaves, texting each other like high school kids.

They had everything going for them. They shared a sense of humor, an ability to spend time together without having to fill every second if they chose not to do it, shared an interest in books, loved sci-fi, and sports. Even the differences in their personalities only seemed to add interest to the total package.

The hardest thing about being with Ali was not reaching out, taking her in his arms, and kissing her. He backed off that except for *hello* and *good night.* He wanted her to know that he respected her, in addition to everything else he felt about her. So he smiled when she smiled and brushed the hair from her face, all the while wondering when the time would be right.

But in doing so, was he sending the wrong signal? In his attempt to let her know this time was different, could he also have backed too far away?

He hoped not, because this time he wanted it all. For the first time in his life he wanted someone to share it with.

Love was more work than his military job. But Ali was worth the effort.

Of that he had no doubt as he had the cab drop him off at the entrance to the New Jersey Convention Center in Edison. Davis was picking him up out front in two hours, and then it was off to the air show for the weekend. He would have rather spent it with Ali, but it was a commitment he made before he met her. Besides, there was this Green Fest thing she had to do for work.

He looked up at the banner hanging over the entrance. Good thing he didn't wear camouflage and draw attention to his career. To show up like that would be like wearing a bathing suit at the North Pole.

He paid the entrance fee and looked around. How hard could it be to find a five-foot-six-inch penguin?

Only ten minutes remained in the morning photo session, and the line of kids waiting to get a picture with Bundles the Recycling Penguin was finally getting shorter. Ali put her flippers on the shoulders of a little boy with a Mets cap and waited until the volunteer nodded. In minutes, the printer spit out a color four-by-six shot, and the volunteer handed it to the boy's mother.

She had probably taken a hundred pictures with kids of assorted sizes, families, and school trip classes. And it wasn't even noon yet.

"Almost done," the volunteer said as she positioned a family around Ali.

Ali nodded, the large penguin head bouncing on her shoulders. One of the kids started pulling the costume while another tried to look inside the head through the air screen inside the oversized smiling mouth. Calmly, Ali gestured to the camera, hoping the mother would pick up on the body language.

"Look at the camera," she heard the mom say as she stilled and waited for the next shot.

"Have time for one more?" she heard a familiar voice say.

She almost knocked over the recycling backdrop when she turned to it. "Jake," she shouted to be sure he heard her, "what are you doing here?"

"I wanted to see what you do to save the planet."

She struck an exaggerated pose and pointed to the

recycling symbol on the photo backdrop with her right flipper. "It's a job." She started to remove the penguin head. Jake reached up and helped her take it off. Once free, she shook her head to get the hair off her neck. "Thanks. It's pretty warm in there."

"How much more time do you have on duty?" Jake asked.

"I'm actually done until about two, and then we do more pictures until four."

Jake turned to the volunteer. "Do you have time for one more shot?" He swiveled his head back toward Ali. "I don't have a picture of you."

"Not like this," Ali said, slipping the black felt flipper-gloves from her hands before running her fingers through her damp hair. "I look like someone who should be on the Discovery Channel's medical mystery show—Ali Archer, half-human, half-bird."

Jake's mouth curved in a smile and his forefinger traced her cheek. "I think you look beautiful."

She could see by the emotion in his eyes that he meant it. "Take two," she told the volunteer, her gaze staying on Jake when the first picture was snapped.

"How about looking at the camera for one?" she heard the volunteer say.

Jake wrapped an arm around Ali and they turned in unison to the camera.

"Perfect," the volunteer said. "The pictures will be out in a minute."

Ali set the *Be Back In* sign to 2 P.M. while Jake got the photos. "Let me see," she said when he came back. "I look like a freak of nature," she said.

"You do not."

"All you see is a black oval shape with a head."

Jake took the pictures from her. "I don't look that bad, do I?"

She smacked his arm. "I mean me."

"I told you, you're beautiful."

"You think I'm beautiful in *this?*"

"Don't argue. Pick one."

She took the one in which they we facing each other. She liked the way they held each other's eyes. "I didn't have a picture of you either," she said tucking it into the tote bag she brought with her. "How did you find me?"

"How many human penguins could there be in Central Jersey?" he asked her.

"This weekend there's just one. I thought you were at the air show."

"I will be in about two hours. I have to meet Tom Davis outside in a couple of hours. He's driving us down. But I wanted to see you first."

Ali felt herself warm and she knew it wasn't because she was still wearing the costume. Jake's thoughtful gesture was as unexpected as it was welcomed.

"I could use something to drink after being in this costume for two hours," Ali said. "How about I sneak you into the staff room and you help me out of this thing?"

Jake raised his eyebrows up and down suggestively. "It depends on what you're wearing underneath it."

"I'm wearing jeans and a tee shirt."

"I was hoping for a bikini."

"Sorry to disappoint you," Ali said with a shrug.

"Actually, you won't. If I remember correctly, it was

your jeans that drew my attention to you in the first place."

Ali wrinkled her brow. "You liked my jeans?"

He took hold of her hand. "It's a very interesting story, and I should probably tell you before you meet Davis, because if I don't there's no telling how he will embellish it."

Ali stepped back as far as his handhold would allow and gave him a wary look. "This I've got to hear."

Jake nodded. "And it's best you hear it from me, so lead the way."

"Sure, but you're carrying the head."

Ali led Jake to the back part of the hall, to a door that said *Staff Only.* Once inside, they found a bare-bones meeting room with cafeteria-style tables and chairs. Against one wall was a table that had some coffee, other drinks, and assorted snacks. They grabbed some bottled water on the way to chairs near the only window.

Jake pulled out one of the chairs and set the headpiece on it while Ali unfastened some Velcro and stepped out of the costume. He patted the head. "I gather this thing attracts a lot of attention."

Ali folded the costume and put it next to the headpiece. "I know how Mickey Mouse feels at Disney World. When the kids see Bundles, it's a mad rush. Sometimes I barely hold my own and feel like I'm going to end up on the ground on my butt looking up at twenty pairs of eyes."

Jake laughed. "That would be a sight."

"It is. I've seen it happen." She unscrewed the cap from her water bottle and took a long drink. "I know why I'm here, and I know I'm irresistible, but why are you really here? I'm not complaining," she quickly added.

"I could say something flip, like 'I couldn't wait to kiss you again,' but we're not supposed to be doing that. I believe you said something about it being distracting."

"Under certain circumstances, it is very distracting," she agreed.

She looked into his incredible eyes and nearly drowned in the emotion she saw there. How easy it would be for her to jump up and lean into his muscled body and give him a welcome kiss. But she wouldn't do that. She wouldn't be caught up in the heat, not without the heart. And she just didn't think he had had enough time with her to know which he felt.

"I came here just because I like to see you, Ali." He leaned forward and slid his forearms onto the table, hands clasped.

His words broke her thoughts. "I like to see you, too, Jake."

"Were you surprised?"

"Yes, I was—to say the least. But I was also happy to see you. This Green Fest is taking up two days out of the nine you have left."

"That sounds like you might miss me."

She reached out and slid her fingers between his hands. "I may, a little." He moved his hands so they held hers. "But that all depends on what you have to tell me about my jeans."

"I was hoping you'd forgotten," Jake admitted.

"I never forget anything. So, what's wrong with them?"

"There's absolutely nothing wrong with them. And that's the problem."

Ali's brows pulled into a frown. "You are the most confusing man I have ever met."

Grinning carelessly, Jake traced the edges of her hand with his fingertips. "Do you remember the day we met?"

"How can I ever forget? You tricked me."

"That's a point of debate for later."

Ali saw the devilry in Jake's eyes. "And I won't forget to bring that up either. Go on."

"Davis drove me to the party that day. When we turned the corner, he saw you back at the trunk of your car." He paused and saw that Ali had the "continue" look on her face, so he did, as gently as he could possibly think to do. "You were bending over inside the trunk." He paused again. "You were in a pair of tight jeans." This time he saw Ali's eyes widen when the concept hit her.

"The first impression you had of me was my backside?"

Her eyes remained as large as saucers while she waited for the answer, and Jake couldn't tell if it was anger or humor he saw run rampant in them.

He tread as cautiously as he could. "There's a little more to it."

She snickered. "Do go on."

"You have to understand that there isn't a whole lot

to do in the sandbox. We invent things to occupy our time."

"What kind of things?" Ali asked suspiciously.

"We make up games."

"What kind of games are they?"

Jake gripped her hand more tightly. "A lot of times, they're betting-type games."

Her eyes finally narrowed. "And just what did you bet?"

Jake flinched. "I bet that I could get a date with you."

Ali pursed her lips. "Well, I guess you won."

Ali shot him a look that Jake thought just might be able to turn back the tide. "Or did I actually lose?" he asked awkwardly.

"Oh, you won," Ali replied with a most unlady-like snort. "And exactly what was it that you won?"

"It was kind of open-ended," Jake admitted. "It wasn't so much that I won, but rather that Tom lost."

Ali nodded her understanding. "So, this bet was a macho man-thing."

"You know guys," Jake said with a shrug meant to signal his surrender.

"Let me get this straight," Ali continued. "You made a bet on my backside and didn't even bother to make sure you won something tangible."

"I guess you could say something like that."

"I could say *something* like that, or *exactly* like that?"

"I'd say that depends on which one is not going to get me killed."

"You're an idiot."

Jake nodded. "Yes, it seems so."

It was at the point Ali couldn't hold back any longer. She burst out laughing. "The least you could have done was gotten money for dinner or something."

Jake leaned back in the chair. "You're not mad?" He seemed amazed.

"You were going to meet me anyway," Ali said. "We were going to the same party."

"But I didn't know that at the time."

"And I do have a rather nice backside."

Jake nodded again. "That I do know."

Ali's eyes narrowed in a playful warning. "My mama always told me that when you're in a hole, you should probably stop digging."

"Your mama is a very smart woman."

They laughed together.

Jake picked up her hand a placed a kiss on it. "Other women might be mad."

"I'm not other women."

"I am well aware of that fact."

He watched her lips part and saw a vulnerability come into her eyes. "Plus I don't have the luxury of having time to be angry at you. You're leaving in a few days." She got up from the chair and walked to his side of the table. "Now I'll take a kiss as an apology."

When he stood and looked into her eyes, the words *I love you* almost came out of her mouth. But she swallowed them. She didn't know what he would do if he knew how she felt about him. She had about a week to help him decide, and she certainly wasn't going to spend any of it on being angry about a stupid bet she was happy that he had won.

So, instead, she surrendered to his arms and kissed him with an intensity she hoped would begin to let him know she didn't intend to be the next girl he left behind.

"Jake Daultry, meet your party at the reception area."

The voice made Jake look at his watch. "Two hours sure went by fast."

Ali gestured to the loudspeaker hanging on the wall. "How did your friend get someone to do that?"

"The loudspeaker voice was distinctly feminine, and Tom is distinctly male," Jake replied.

"Is he a player?"

Jake laughed. "He thinks he is."

"I think I need to meet the man who brought us together," Ali said, looking at her watch, "but it's nearly time for the next round of pictures. I hope you don't mind walking out with a life-sized penguin."

Jake picked up the headpiece. "I wouldn't have it any other way."

They walked to the reception area and saw a dark-haired man leaning on the counter. By the look on the face of the woman behind the desk, he was making some brownie points of his own. As they got closer, they saw he was holding her hand and could hear his line. "I will remember your eyes forever," he was telling her.

"Davis, leave the nice lady alone," Jake said when he was next to his friend.

Davis dropped the young woman's hand and turned to Jake. He looked Ali up and down. "So, you're dating mascots now?" he quipped.

"I think I'll let the penguin handle that answer," Jake said, stepping back with a flourish.

Ali took off the headpiece. "I guess you didn't recognize me." She turned and shook her tail feathers. "But maybe that's because I'm not wearing blue jeans."

Davis laughed and turned to Jake. "You're a brave man, Daultry, to tell her about the bet." He turned back to Ali. "So, Lady Blue Jeans, do you have a name?"

"My name is Ali—Ali Archer."

He held out his hand. "I'm Tom—Tom Davis." He smiled when she shook it warmly. "Well then, Miss Ali," he continued, "I have to say you are the best-looking penguin I've ever seen."

About that time they heard squeals coming from across the room.

"It's Bundles!" a small voice shouted.

"I want a picture," another said.

"I want one first."

They turned and saw a group of about twenty school-children coming toward them. Ali quickly put the head-piece back on.

"I have to get back to work," she said as the first child reached her. "Call me."

"I will," Jake said as the rest of the kids caught up and surrounded her. The voices blended into one big shriek as they pulled her off in the direction of the photo booth. "I love you, Ali," he called out, not knowing if she would hear him.

Did she really hear what she thought she heard?

Ali tried to turn around, but was stopped by twenty

small bodies pulling on her flippers and pushing her toward the photo booth from behind. She was helpless to do anything but continue forward.

Sure, her head was stuffed into an oversized penguin costume, and the delighted screeches of second graders kind of got caught in the huge empty space surrounding her head, but she could have sworn she heard Jake's voice among all the shrieking saying that he loved her. When she was finally able to turn around, though, he was gone.

As she raised her right flipper to pose for the first picture, she knew she couldn't be certain of that. But one thing she did know: There was no way he was going back to Iraq without her finding out for sure.

Chapter Fifteen

"You have barely said anything since you got in the car," Tom Davis said as he eased his car into the traffic on Route one on his way to Trenton. "You won the bet. You should be ecstatic."

"It was a stupid bet," Jake declared.

"Maybe it was, but you got to meet this girl."

"I would have met her anyway. It turns out she's my cousin's sister-in-law, and we were going to the same party."

"But you have to admit, I made it happen sooner." Davis glanced over at Jake. "What have you got there?"

Jake held up the picture taken at the photo booth. "It's a picture of me and Ali."

Davis reached over and snatched it out of Jake's hand. "Let me see." He held it between the thumb and forefinger of his right hand and steered the car with his left, taking quick glances at it as he watched the road ahead. "She is cute, even wrapped up in that costume she was wearing."

Jake took it back. "She works for the county recycling department." He laughed. "She's saving the planet one can at a time."

Davis lifted his chin. "Oh, she's a tree hugger."

"Be respectful. She's very passionate about her job," Jake insisted. "And the environment is important. We do kind of wreak havoc with it while we do ours."

"Hum, sounds like Lady Blue Jeans has made an impression on you."

"Her name's Ali."

"Wow, this is more serious than I thought," Davis said, clicking on the left-side blinker and pulling into the fast lane to pass a tractor-trailer.

"You bet it is," Jake agreed. The sudden catch in his voice surprised him, as did the emotions following on the heels of his telling Ali he loved her right before he left the convention center. It was a spontaneous reaction, something he never did.

"Does she feel the same?"

Jake shrugged. "I don't know."

"What do you mean, you don't know? I heard you tell the woman that you loved her. If she didn't know before, she does now."

The obvious observation made Jake take a long, slow, deep breath. "I have this all screwed up, Tom."

"How so?"

"I told her about Carly."

Davis nodded, a smile breaking out across his face. "Ah, yes, I remember Good-Time Carly." He then reached over with his right hand and smacked Jake on the head. "Telling the new lady about the last lady is a definite no-no if you want to progress in the early stages of a relationship."

"So you're an expert in relationships now."

"No, but not crossing that line is in the super-secret-spit-on-your-palm-and-shake man-code book."

"Sorry, I didn't read it."

"That could be excused, but you did leave the woman you just told that you loved in a room full of people while you hopped into a car to go to an air show."

"That I did," Jake admitted, nodding thoughtfully.

"And that's not exactly the tone I would want to set early on. Is she coming to the air show later?"

Jake shook his head. "No, she has to work at the Green Fest for the entire weekend."

"But you two have discussed the endless possibilities of exploring the wonders of life and love, right?"

Jake grimaced. "Well, we haven't exactly used those words."

"Okay, but then you have talked about talking about it when you get back from the sandbox."

Jake shook his head again. "Not exactly, we haven't."

"You know we're leaving in a week, right?"

"I'm well aware of that," Jake said.

"And you love a woman you haven't really told properly, and you're leaving her in a world of civilians who could charm the heck out of her while you are AWOL from her life."

"Davis, you are a master of the obvious."

Davis shook his head. "Let me tell you what else is obvious, my man."

By the look on Davis' face, Jake knew whatever he

was about to say wasn't going to be good. "And what would that be?" Jake asked cautiously.

Davis turned his head fully toward Jake. "It would be that you are totally screwed unless you do something fast."

As soon as the Green Fest closed for the night, Ali stuffed the Bundles costume in the trunk of her car and headed to her mom's house. Once there, she threw open the car door and tore up the front steps.

"Mom, where are you?" she shouted as soon as she opened the front door.

"I'm in the kitchen," was the reply. "And what's with all the noise?"

Ali found her mother getting a cup of freshly brewed coffee. "You have to help me," Ali declared going to straight to the cabinet and getting out her favorite mug.

"That's what mothers do, dear," Tess replied, getting the milk from the refrigerator and setting the carton on the table. "What kind of mess have you gotten yourself into this time?"

Ali pulled out a chair and sat at the table. "It's not a mess, Mom. It's more like a situation." She slid her mug toward her mother.

Tess filled it with coffee. "What kind of situation is it?" She sat down next to Ali. "And what can I do to help you?"

Ali threaded a hand through her hair. "Do you really believe in love at first sight, Mom?"

"You asked me that already. My answer hasn't changed."

Ali's hand gripped her mug tighter and she looked down into the dark liquid. "Then whatever you had, I caught." She looked up at the mother. "I think I'm in love with Jake."

Tess clasped her hands together. "That is wonderful."

"Don't get too excited, Mom. He doesn't know."

"You haven't told him?"

Ali shook her head.

"Why haven't you?" Tess asked. She saw Ali lower her eyes. "Oh, he doesn't feel the same."

Ali's eyes came back to her mother's. "No, he does. At least, I think he does."

"Did he tell you that?"

"I think so."

Tess reached over and took her daughter's hand. "Telling someone that you love them either happens or it doesn't. There is nothing to think about at all."

Ali took a steadying breath. There was no point beating around the bush, not with her mother. So she launched right into it.

"I'm working the Green Fest this weekend, and Jake has something to do at the air show. We didn't think we'd see each other until Sunday night. But he came to see me at the convention center. I have to be Bundles, so when he was leaving, a whole bunch of kids came running at me and they were all screaming and laughing, and that's when I thought I heard him tell me that he loved me." She finally took another breath. "But it could have been one of the kids, so I really can't be sure." There, it was out. Ali felt both relieved and anxious as she waited for her mother's reaction. She took a deep breath and then looked at her mother. Tess was smiling.

"There's only one way to be sure, dear," she heard her mother say. "You have to ask him."

"But what if I heard wrong? I would feel like such a doofus."

Tess squeezed her daughter's hand. "Do you love him?"

Ali closed her eyes and held her breath. "Yes," she said in a rush of air.

"Then you should tell him that."

"So, should I confess that I love him before or after I ask him if he said it first?"

"It doesn't matter what you heard or think you heard. If you love someone, you should tell them."

Ali face crinkled with a grin. Her mother was right. She was always right. "You're my size, right?" she asked her mother.

"I think so," Tess replied.

Ali got up from the chair. "How do you feel about penguins?"

Chapter Sixteen

In theory, her plan had been perfect. One stop at home, and then it was on to the air show to find Jake. But when traffic slowed to a crawl about a mile from the entrance to the base, Ali had her doubts. Even at this late hour, visitors were still on their way in to see the remaining attractions at the air show. Soldiers and airmen acting as parking lot attendants patiently directed the late arrivals to parking slots. She could either walk or take a shuttle to the airfield.

After securing a seat on the bus, she took a few minutes to try to reach Jake on his cell phone. She suspected he wouldn't have it on, but she left him a text message anyway. Then she slipped her phone into an outside pocket of her purse, not knowing if she would hear it ring. Noise from aircraft of all types filled the air.

A short five-minute ride later, the bus unloaded its passengers at the gate to the airfield. Ali looked around, taking in the sheer size of it, not to mention the thousands of visitors milling around. She felt a brief *Where's Waldo?*-moment before shaking off the scope of the task.

Unless her cell phone rang and it was Jake on the other end, she had a long night ahead of her. But Jake was here somewhere, and she wasn't about to leave until she found him.

The sound of jet engines grew louder, and Ali looked up to see some old planes flying in formation toward the airstrip. They looked like they could have been from the fifties, single propeller on the nose, low wings, oval cockpit, and short tail. Still they flew in perfect formation toward the late day sun. Ali shielded her eyes with her hand and stopped walking, watching as if connected, as they began trailing some sort of smoke from behind them. Everyone walking with her to the airfield stopped and began to applaud.

The voice over a loudspeaker announced that the planes were the Skywriters, an air-demonstration team flying World War II-era planes. The voice also announced that the Thunderbirds, the premier Air Force demonstration team, would have about thirty minutes left in their ground show, after which the F-16's would roll out for the night.

She dug the ticket Jake had given her out of her purse and looked around. Inside the gate, it seemed to her the crowds had tripled somehow. It would take a small miracle to find Jake in the short time left before she had to leave the base for the night.

The next announcement gave her hope. The announcer said that the Black Hawk helicopters would be leaving in fifteen minutes for an auxiliary airfield, and that visitors needed to take their final pictures. Ali's face brightened. That's where Jake would be.

She snaked her way quickly through the crowd until she found someone she thought might be able to help. "Where are the Black Hawks?" she asked a young airman standing a parade rest next to a table filled with information on the military.

He pointed to the left. "Go to the end of the line of tents. You can't miss them. But you have to hurry, ma'am. They're about to leave."

"Not before I get there," Ali vowed.

"The Black Hawk replaces the Huey-Iroquois," Jake said to a group of people who had gathered. "It's the only helicopter to fly in all five branches of the military."

"You know how to fly it?" a boy of about six asked.

Jake dropped to one knee. "I sure do. It's my job."

"That's cool," the boy said.

"Oh, yeah, that's very cool," Ali repeated.

Jake's head whipped around. "Ali, it's you!" His face registered both pleasure and surprise. "What are you doing here?"

"I wanted to see you."

"Am I in trouble?" he asked.

She could tell by the tone of his voice he was concerned. "I don't think so. Finish what you're doing here, and then I'll tell you," she said with a wink.

Jake smiled his agreement and turned back to the boy.

While Ali waited for him, she watched him. He treated each question as if it were the most important of the day, and each person with whom he interacted as though he or she was the only person within miles. It was his gift, she decided. He could make anyone feel special. He had done that for her.

Each time she was with him, she felt complete, like Jake had stepped into a part of her she had reserved just for him. When he was away from her, she counted the hours until they could be together. Technology came in handy then. She was sure her next cell phone bill was going to be triple figures.

But Jake's perfect actions also underscored her fears. He had been trained to be perfect by the military. She could not help but wonder if that training spilled over into his personal life.

Either way, she had to find out if he really loved her. And just like in the military, timing would be everything. If she was going to play the fool, she would do it at a time of her choosing.

And it would be sometime tonight.

The urgency to talk to Ali occupied Jake's mind during the rest of his time of volunteer duty. It gnawed at his patience as he stood for the final pictures. It wasn't like him. But then again, nothing in his life seemed the same since he'd met Ali.

He looked over at her as the flight crew prepared the Black Hawks to leave for the auxiliary field. He liked the pale blue blouse she wore. It brought out the unbelievable range of blue tones in her eyes. The setting sun framed her with its halo of light, making her look like the angel she was to him. How in the world was he going to be able to let her go?

"We're ready, sir," he heard one of the crewman call out.

Jake turned to Ali. "Do you want a ride?"

Ali's eyes widened and she pointed to the helicopter. "Do you mean in that?" She looked at him. "I thought you said they were fired on. Is it safe?"

"Yep, all systems are go." Jake put his hand on the small of her back and guided her to the pad. "The major repairs have been done. There's only some minor work left, none of it that affects flying."

"Won't you get in trouble?"

"I don't think so. It's not like we're going to be flying a mission. We're just going over to the next airfield."

Ali grinned. "Then let's go."

He helped her into the seat beside the pilot's, and one of the grounds crew helped her stick the lap belt and two shoulder harnesses into a single circular lock.

Jake handed her foam ear plugs. "Put these in and then put the headset on."

"Will I need all this?" Ali asked, taking the gear from him.

"You bet you will."

She watched Jake don the war protection and she did the same. Whether it helped or not, she couldn't tell, because after a pre-flight check, he started the engine. A low-pitched cyclical growl turned into a full-throated roar as the rotors started turning. The decibels mounted with every revolution until everything else was inaudible except for the whomp-whomp-whomp of air being sliced by helicopter blades. She looked out over the helicopter pad. The grounds lights were on, and against the darkening sky, everything seemed surreal.

Jake reached over and tapped her on the shoulder. When she turned to him, he gave her the signal that he was about to take off. She shot him back a thumbs-up, telling him that she was ready. Then they were up, the helicopter shuddering as it gained elevation.

Ali held on to the seat with both hands. She had never experienced anything like this. In the dusky light she could see roofs with satellite dishes, and beyond the sprawl of the base, the neatly groomed lawns with the box-style homes of the base housing.

The Black Hawk dipped and swayed. At one moment, Jake flew it parallel to the ground, and in another, he jerked it to one side, rolling into a forty-five-degree angle. Ali turned to him and grinned to let him know that she wasn't scared.

It seemed to only take a few seconds when the airfield came into sight. A pattern of lights ringed the landing pad, and crewmen waited for Jake to land.

As the copter descended tail-first, Ali noticed for the first time one of the reasons the Black Hawk was in for repairs. The bright light of the landing lights on the pad sent white beams through what could only be bullet holes in the helicopter's metal skin. She turned toward Jake, intent on gesturing to them, when what she saw almost stopped her heart.

There was a beam of light coming through one of the holes and settling on Jake's shoulder. This must have been the Black Hawk he was piloting when he'd gotten hurt. Ali's lips parted and her mouth went dry. All her fears played out in front of her widened eyes.

Jake looked from Ali's eyes to his shoulder. He could not land the helicopter fast enough.

"Don't cry, honey." Jake's arms enveloped her as soon as she ripped the safety harness free. His embrace made her feel safe. But even as he kissed her forehead, her hair, her cheeks, and murmured words of comfort, her mind could not erase the sight of the field lights shining through the bullet holes in the helicopter, the rays landing on Jake. It underscored how fragile life could be and her need to make sure she spent the rest of it with him.

"I should have thought that out better," Jake said.

She pulled back slightly. Her gaze lowered to his shoulder, and she lightly touched the spot where she had seen the light rise through the bullet hole. "That was your helicopter, wasn't it?"

Jake nodded, his chin nudging her hair as he did. "I'm sorry," he croaked.

Ali pulled in a shaky breath. "It's okay."

His arms tightened around her as though he was afraid she would run off.

"You could have been killed," she said sniffling against his chest, her tears wetting his shirt.

"It's a price some of us have to pay for freedom, Ali." She felt his hand move to her hair. He stroked it gently as he spoke. "We all take that chance every day. It's no different for you crossing the street." He kissed the top of her head. "It comes with being alive."

"I couldn't stand it if I lost you," Ali said with a sniffle.

"You'll never lose me unless it's what you want," he whispered against her cheek before gently placing a kiss there. "But that would kill me as surely as any bullet. Since I met you a few weeks ago, I can't imagine being with anyone else." Tenderly, he ran his thumb across her cheek, loving the warm feeling, loving her so much he almost hurt to breathe. His throat constricted but somehow he found the words. "So where does this leave us?"

Ali closed her eyes and took a steadying breath. She pulled back from him as much as his arms would allow. This was the time. She took a deep breath to gather her fleeting courage and began, "At the Green Fest when you were leaving, I thought I heard you say something."

Jake nodded. "What did you think you heard?"

"I think you said that you loved me."

His face broke into a smile. "I did. I wake up thinking about you, and I go to sleep dreaming about you."

A sob caught in Ali's throat. She reached up and framed his face with her hands. "Then I have to talk to you," she said with a sniffle.

Jake heard the waver in her voice. "Should we sit down first?"

"I think we had better."

There was a bench outside the hanger, and he led her to it. She could see the wariness in his eyes when she turned to him as they sat. He took her hands in his and looked down at them briefly before returning his gaze to her face.

"You're dumping me, aren't you?" His voice was low and controlled.

Ali didn't know whether to laugh or cry. A wave of

relief flooded her. Apparently they were both worried about the same thing.

Her words came out in a rush of air. "You can't get rid of me because you're going back to Iraq. I mean, I suppose you can, and maybe you even should so you won't be distracted while you work, but I don't want you to." She sniffled. "I know I'm being selfish, but I don't want you dancing in the sand with nurses or thinking about anyone else when there's down time." Her voice dropped to a whisper. "I know why you might want to—I really do, but—" She stopped. Did she even have the right to ask this?

In response, Jake hugged her more tightly. "Forget what happened before. It wasn't right." He kissed her forehead. "This is."

She stopped him with a forefinger to his lips. "Let me finish before I lose my nerve." She took a calming breath. "I tried to make sense of everything. I didn't believe Mom when she told me, but she was right. Leonard did say it's a chemical thing in the brain, so you can't control it. I didn't believe him either, until now."

Jake's brows furrowed. "Who is Leonard?"

"He's a rocket scientist, so he knows everything. He said it's like F plus M equals C, or something like that. I wrote it all down on a napkin. I have it at home if you want to see it."

Jake's expression didn't change when he asked, "You're breaking up with me because of a rocket scientist and algebra?"

"No, I'm telling you that I love you because of a rocket scientist and algebra." She touched his lips with her fingertips. "I simply love you." Then she held what was left of the breath and waited.

With a groan, Jake held her even more tightly. "I love you so darn much, Ali. I think I loved you from the day I met you. You're the most important thing in my life. How you managed to do that in three weeks, I don't know, nor do I care. I just want you in my life forever."

Ali wiped her eyes. "But I'm afraid, Jake."

He kissed her temple. "Of what?"

"Of being a distraction to you when you're over there. I have to know you'll focus on the missions and not me. I'd never forgive myself if something happened to you."

"You've been number one in my heart since that day I saw your jeans," Jake began. The comment made Ali laugh, and it buoyed him. "But when I'm flying, be assured I'm very focused on my job. I'm career Army. That's the way it will have to be if I'm going to come home in once piece. And I will be coming home—to you, if you'll have me."

Ali would have nothing less. "Then I have one more request to make before you go."

"And what would that be?"

"Marry me."

Jake beamed. "Just as soon as I get back."

"That won't work," Ali said, shaking her head.

Jake drew down his brows guardedly. "You just asked me to marry you and I accepted. Are you changing your mind?"

"I'm not changing my mind—just the time. Marry me now." She looked at her watch. "If you're not doing anything, marry me today if we can get a flight."

Chapter Seventeen

Jake and Ali sat in the back of the Chapel of the Velvet Elvis in Las Vegas waiting their turn. The chapel's interior was decorated much like the living room at Graceland, complete with stained glass panels of peacocks, mirrored walls, heavy gold drapes, ornate white furniture, white walls, and gold trim.

The preacher, an Elvis impersonator looking a lot like him in a white spangled jumpsuit complete with cape and scarf, even had the accent down. "Now by the power vested in me by the great state of Nevada, I pronounce you husband and wife," he said with the signature Elvis lip-curl. "Thank you—thank you very much."

The newlyweds kissed as the organist, who tried but failed to resemble Priscilla, played "Love Me Tender" as they exited.

Ali puffed out her cheeks and let out the air in short, choppy breaths. She tapped her nails on the armrest in time to the music as the next couple walked to the preacher.

"You don't have to go through with this," Jake whispered, noticing her nervousness. He gestured to three more couples waiting their turn. "Elvis has plenty of business today, and I'm sure we won't be the first people who changed their minds."

"You want to change your mind?"

His eyes told her his answer before he said it. "No, I don't. I just want to give you an opportunity to run in case you don't want to be married to a military man."

"I'm not running anywhere," she assured him.

Jake saw her smile soften and her eyes light with an emotion he knew would always be there. "Then neither am I."

"I always knew I would marry you, Jake," Ali continued, holding his gaze steady so he would know she meant every word of what she was about to say. "I didn't know what you would look like on the outside, but I recognized you on the inside almost from the first day. You're honest, committed, caring. You listen before you react to what I do, and you are willing to compromise. You let me be the person I am, and you don't try to change me. How could anyone want more from someone except to spend the rest of her life with him?"

"I hardly know how to answer that, except that I love you for exactly the same reasons." Now it was his turn to be sure she knew he loved her with everything that he was. He took her hand. "I know I upset you when I told you about the last time I left for overseas."

Ali lowered her eyes.

Before she could say anything, Jake placed his fingertips under her chin and raised it. "But as sure as I know you and I are right together, I knew *that* wasn't. I love you, Ali. I have no doubts, no fears, and I will never have any regrets if we let Elvis up there do his thing."

She reached up and tugged on a short veil she'd purchased at a local bridal shop on the way to the chapel. "I'd hate to waste a perfectly good twenty-dollar bridal veil." She looked down at her jeans. "Maybe I should have bought a dress too."

Jake shook his head. "No way, your jeans brought us together, and your jeans need to commemorate the beginning of our life together."

Ali looked off into the distance and bit down on her lower lip.

"I guess if you want a dress that badly, we can always run out and get one and come back," he quickly added.

"No, we're not losing our place in line. I was just organizing, that's all."

"What do you mean, you were organizing?"

"I have to make sure Mom does Bundles tomorrow, and then I have to call Diana and arrange for next week off. Oh, and we should grab a few more of those coupons we saw on the table outside—you know, the ones for half off a room at the Excalibur." She winked. "We need a honeymoon."

Jake laughed and drew her into his arms. "I would be happy to be your knight in shining armor. But don't expect us to get to the all-you-can-eat buffet too much."

Ali rested her cheek against his. "Room service will be fine."

The next couple finished their vows, and the Priscilla look-alike motioned for Ali and Jake.

"Well, this is it. It's your last chance to change your mind," Jake told her.

Ali stood. "Let's get married, G.I. Joe."

"Tree Hugger," Jake replied, taking her hand and grinning.

"That's about-to-become Mrs. G.I. Joe instead, if you don't mind."

Halfway up to Elvis, Jake suddenly stopped. "Ali, we need a ring. This happened so fast, I don't have a ring for you."

"But I do." She reached into the pocket of her jeans and pulled out a gold band with six small citrine stones set in a line. "I went home and got it before I drove to the air show. I'd like to think that Gran whispered in my ear and told me that I might need it today." She handed it to him.

Jake let it fall into the palm of his hand. "So, this is the infamous Grandmother's Ring."

Ali nodded. "My Grandmother was born in November. My grandfather gave it to her the first year they met." She grinned. "Gran always said it was love at first sight with him. Guess that's a family thing too."

"I promise I'll get you a real wedding ring when I get back. We can pick it out together."

Ali picked up the ring from Jake's hand. "I kind of like this one. It's a yellow ribbon for my finger, but I may never take it off even when you do come home. I guess Mom was right about the rings helping us find our soul mates, after all." She handed the citrine ring back to Jake. "Shall we?"

"Let's."

He cocked his elbow and Ali slipped her hand around it. He put his free hand over hers, and together they walked the last few steps toward Elvis and their new life together.

For Ali, this was her dream wedding. It didn't matter that she was wearing blue jeans instead of a beautiful white gown; it only mattered that she would be taking her vows with Jake.

As for her mother, she knew Tess enjoyed being the mother of the bride for Somer and would enjoy being the mother of the groom for Trent in a little over six weeks.

For this wedding, though, Tess would just have to settle for a picture with Elvis.

Epilogue

Almost six months later

"Okay, we're all here. What's up?" Trent and Linda, married three months now, walked into Tess's house. Ali, Somer, and Nick were already there.

"Jake is going to call via the Internet," Ali said, booting up her mother's laptop. She moved some chairs to the table. "Gather around, and don't forget to stay near the center of the screen when you're talking to him so the camera will catch your image when you talk."

"He's been doing that about once a month since he left. Why'd we all have to be here?" Trent asked, settling in around the table.

"We're planning Ali and Jake's real wedding," Tess explained.

"Wouldn't that be better done once he's home?" Trent asked.

Michael crawled over and tugged on his uncle's pants. Trent picked him up from the floor. "What have you been feeding this guy?" he asked. "He's getting heavy."

"He's growing," Somer retorted. "He's almost a year old. He'll be walking soon, so he'll thin out."

Trent bounced his nephew on his knee with Linda cooing at the little boy over Trent's shoulder. "I hope so, otherwise you'll have to get him a trainer."

Somer handed her son an Oreo cookie. "Here, munchkin—eat this, and show Uncle Trenton how you can turn his nice, new T-shirt into a napkin." She turned to Linda and mouthed the word *sorry.*

Linda dismissed the apology with a swipe of her hand. "Don't worry about it. Trent deserves it."

"All of you, stop it," Tess insisted, bringing out a pitcher of iced tea. "Try to get along while we wait for Jake to call. We do have a reception to plan for after Jake comes home."

Almost on cue, the call connected and Jake appeared on the laptop screen.

"Hi, honey," Ali said as soon as she saw his face.

"Hi, baby. Is everyone there?"

"They sure are," Ali assured him.

"Hey, cuz, how's it going?" Nick chimed in.

"So are you still burning a hole in the ozone layer with jet fuel?" Trent asked. Ali smacked her brother's shoulder in response, while everyone there made sure they got in their greetings.

"We were just talking about the reception Mom is planning," Ali said once all the pleasantries were exchanged. "She wants us to renew our vows at church too."

"Tess, you don't trust Elvis?" Jake asked with a laugh.

"Elvis was fine, a little bit of a shock, you understand, but fine," Tess replied as Trent and Somer made agreeing faces.

"Mom thinks we might like a wedding with attendants and a flower girl," Ali chimed in.

Jake grinned. "Did you tell her that we had a flower girl in mind for just that kind of occasion?"

"I thought we could tell her together," Ali said. She put her hand on top of the monitor and turned to her family. "Jake and I know of someone we are sure is going to be perfect."

"Who's that, dear?" her mother asked. "Jessica, your cousin Barbara's little girl? She's about five. She would be perfect."

Ali shook her head. "No, the girl we're thinking of is named Tessa Janine."

Tess furrowed her brow. "I like her first name, but who is she?"

Ali looked at Jake, who nodded. From her back pocket, Ali pulled out a photo. She held it up. "She's your granddaughter." For a moment, no one moved. Then they all realized Ali was holding up a sonogram picture. "I'm pregnant."

Somer screamed in delight and hugged her sister.

Trent leaned toward the laptop. "You dog, congrats."

"Thanks," Jake said, smiling from ear to ear. He leaned forward, looking at his monitor. "Where's my wife?"

"Right here," Ali said, elbowing her way past Trent and sitting in the center chair in front of the laptop.

"How was the last doctor's visit?" he asked her.

"Great, he says everything is on track for an end of June birth."

Jake looked sad. "I won't be home yet."

Holding the sonogram picture, Tess came into Jake's view. "Don't you worry now. I'll be there to help her. You just stay well and come home safe."

"That I will," Jake agreed. He looked over his shoulder as the PA system went off in the background. "Got to go, babe," he said when he turned back and locked his gaze with Ali's. "I love you." He lowered his gaze to her midsection before returning to her eyes. "I love you both."

"We love you right back," Ali said, tenderly tracing the curve of his face with her forefinger.

"Tell my daughter I'll be dreaming of her," Jake said. "Bye all." Then the screen faded to blue.

Tess hugged her daughter. "I'm getting a granddaughter, Tessa Janine. How wonderful."

"Jake and I are naming her after both her grandmothers." Ali accepted the hugs and good wishes of everyone in room.

"You didn't waste any time getting into the baby thing, did you?" Trent said with a smile.

Ali looked at her mother. "Just like love, babies happen when they happen." She touched her stomach, a loving light coming into her eyes. "She's a honeymoon baby."

"Let me see that picture," Trent said. Tess handed it to him and Trent studied it intently. A grainy black and white picture, it showed a perfectly formed baby. "She looks like you, Ali," he teased.

"Stop it, Trenton," Tess warned. "I'm sure you're happy for your sister and Jake."

"Of course I am," Trent replied. He turned to Ali. "But I'll tell you what, sis. I'll call your baby"—he slapped the sonogram picture down on the table and produced a picture from his back pocket—"and raise you one."

Everyone looked down. It was another sonogram picture. Ali reached over and picked it up. Clearly there were two tiny beings in the center.

"Linda and I are having twins," Trent proudly announced, settling his arm around his wife and patting her stomach. "She's about three months along."

Ali squealed and grabbed Linda, dragging her away from Trent. "We are going to be moms together. I am so happy for you." Then she turned to her brother. "You are such a pain."

Trent feigned surprise. "I'm a pain? Now, why would you say that?"

"You always have to one-up me."

"Hey, I'm a mom too," Somer cut in, not wanting to be left out of the party. "Besides, didn't I start all this?"

Ali and Trent turned in union. "Yes, you did," they both said.

As Somer, Ali, and Trent continued to trade barbs, Tess stepped back and watched it all. As it always seemed to be, her children were loving each other, albeit rather loudly. She would not have it any other way, and she could not be happier.

Somer, her amethyst; Trent, her sapphire; and Ali, her citrine, were all happy, settled, and giving her grandchildren. Her plan had worked to perfection—with a little help from Grandmother's rings.